# DRAKE

## IRON HORSE LEGACY BOOK #6

### ELLE JAMES

TWISTED PAGE INC

# DRAKE

## IRON HORSE LEGACY BOOK #6

*New York Times* & *USA Today*
Bestselling Author

## ELLE JAMES

© date Twisted Page Inc. All rights reserved.

ISBN EBOOK: 978-1-62695-395-6

ISBN PRINT: 978-1-62695-396-3

*Dedicated to my readers who make my dreams come true by keeping me in the business I love dearly...WRITING! I love you all so much. Thank you for buying my books!*
*Elle James*

# AUTHOR'S NOTE

Enjoy other books in this series by Elle James

### *Iron Horse Legacy*
Soldier's Duty (#1)
Ranger's Baby (#2)
Marine's Promise (#3)
SEAL's Vow (#4)
Warrior's Resolve (#5)
Drake (#6)
Grimm (#7)
Murdock (#8)
Utah (#9)
Judge (#10)

Visit ellejames.com for more titles and release dates
Join her newsletter at
https://ellejames.com/contact/

# CHAPTER 1

"Damn," Drake Morgan muttered, checked his speedometer and repeated the expletive.

He hadn't realized he'd been going over the sixty-miles-an-hour speed limit until blue lights flashed in his rearview mirror. Lifting his foot off the accelerator, he slowed and eased to the side of the road, just a few miles from his destination.

A county sheriff's SUV pulled to a stop behind him, and a deputy dropped down from the driver's seat.

The tan, short-sleeved uniform shirt stretched taut over full breasts, the shirt-tails tucked into the waistband of dark brown trousers, cinched around a narrow waist with a thick black belt.

Definitely female. Too petite and pretty to be out patrolling the wild roads of rural Montana.

He lowered the window of his Ford F250 pickup,

reached into his glove box for the vehicle registration and insurance information she'd surely request and straightened.

"Sir, place your hands on the window frame," she said.

He raised his hands, one of which held the documents. The other he carefully placed on the window frame of his door, staring out the open window into the barrel of a pistol. He raised his gaze to the deputy's and cocked an eyebrow. "I have a concealed carry license," he warned. "My weapon is in the glove compartment. I'm unarmed at this moment."

"Just keep your hands where I can see them," she said, her tone curt, her eyes narrowed as she held the pistol pointed at his head.

"Can I ask why I was pulled over?" he asked in a calm, even tone, knowing the answer.

"You were exceeding the speed limit," she said. "If that's your title and registration, I'll take those. But no funny business."

"Trust me," he said with a crooked smile. "I've never been accused of being funny."

Her eyebrows pulled together to form a V over her nose as she took the papers he held out for her.

She studied the documents then glanced up. "You're not from around here," she said.

"No, I'm not," he said.

"Do you know how fast you were going?" she asked, all business, no smile.

Drake almost grinned at the seriousness of the young woman's expression and the way she stiffly held herself. "Over the speed limit?"

She snorted. "By at least fifteen miles an hour. In a hurry to get somewhere?"

"I was."

She shook her head, a hint of a smile tugging at the corners of her mouth. "And how's that working out for you?"

"You tell me," he quipped.

She was pretty in a girl-next-door kind of way with light brown hair pulled back in an efficient ponytail.

Drake stared up into her eyes, trying to decide if they were brown, gold or green, finally settling on hazel. To cap it all, she sported a dusting of freckles on her bare face. "You have my information, but let me introduce myself." He stuck out his hand. "Drake Morgan."

Her brow furrowed as she contemplated his extended hand. "I'm Deputy Douglas." She gave a brief nod, ignored his hand and stared past him into the vehicle. "Since you have a gun in the vehicle with you, you'll need to step out of the truck while I run your data."

Already late for the meeting with his team, their new boss, and this his first day on the job, he sighed, pushed open the door and stepped out with his hands held high.

"Turn around, place your hands on the hood of your vehicle and spread your legs," she said in a tone that brooked no argument.

He cocked an eyebrow. "I'm not a convicted felon. I owned up to the gun in my glove box. I'm unarmed and at your mercy."

Having stated her demand once, she held the gun pointed at his chest, unbending, waiting for him to follow through.

Rather than give her a reason to pull the trigger, he turned and complied with her command.

The shuffle of gravel indicated she'd moved closer. A small, capable hand skimmed over his shoulders, down his sides, around to his abs and lower. Bypassing his private parts, her hand traveled the length of his legs, patting both all the way to his ankles.

Out of the corner of his eye, he watched as she balanced her service weapon with her right hand as she frisked him with her left.

Finally, she straightened and stepped back. "Please stand at the rear of your vehicle while I run your plates and license."

He turned and gave her a twisted grin. "Told you I was unarmed."

She backed toward her vehicle then slipped into the driver's seat. Her fingers danced across a computer keyboard as she entered his license and registration data and waited.

Moments later, she got out of her work vehicle, weapon back in the holster on her belt, and strode toward him while writing on an official-looking pad. When she reached him, she ripped off the top sheet and handed it to him. "I'm only giving you a warning this time. Next time, I'll cite you. Slow it down out there. The life you endanger might not be your own."

With that parting comment, she spun on her booted heels and marched back to her vehicle.

"Deputy Douglas," he called out.

As she opened her SUV, she turned to face him, "Yes, Mr. Morgan?"

"You're the first person I've met here. Nice to meet you." He waved the warning ticket. "And thank you."

Her brow furrowed, and she shook her head as she climbed into the vehicle. Moments later, she passed his truck and continued toward the little town of Eagle Rock ahead of him.

Drake slipped into the driver's seat and followed at a more sedate pace. Hell, he was already late. What were a few more minutes? And it wasn't worth getting a full-fledged ticket. He was lucky she'd only issued a warning. She could've hit him hard with a speeding ticket, with the lasting effect of jacking up his insurance rates.

He owed her a coffee or a beer. Since she was the only person from Eagle Rock he knew besides Hank Patterson, he'd kind of like to get to know her better.

It paid to have the law on your side in these back-water towns.

Following the GPS map on his dash, he drove through town and out the other end, turning on the road leading to his destination.

Soon, he saw her, perched on the side of a mountain, her broad porches intact, her late eighteen-hundred charm shining through, despite the need for a good paint job and dry-rot repair.

The Lucky Lady Lodge clung to the side of the mountain, welcoming travelers in search of a quiet getaway in the Crazy Mountains of Montana.

From what Hank had told him, this lodge had been a place for the gold rush miners of the late eighteen hundreds to spend their hard-earned gold on booze and women.

After the gold had dried up, the Lucky Lady had become a speakeasy during the prohibition, with secret passages into the old mine where they'd made moonshine and stored the contraband in the mountain.

Drake had done some research on the old lodge. He'd found stories telling of days when mafia king-pins had come to conduct business while hunting in the hills or fishing in the mountain streams.

Fires had consumed hundreds of acres surrounding the lodge, missing it on more than one occasion by less than a mile. Throughout the years, the lodge stood as she had from the beginning, a little worn around the edges. Recently, she'd been damaged by an explosion in the mine. That's where Drake and his team would come in.

He looked forward to rolling up his sleeves and putting his carpentry skills to work restoring the old girl. He hoped that, like riding a bike, it would all come back to him despite the sixteen years it had been since he'd last lifted a hammer to build or repair anything more than a deck on the house of a friend. The summers he'd spent working on new home construction while in high school gave him skills he wouldn't have known otherwise and the confidence to try new things he'd never done.

Having joined the Navy straight out of high school, he hadn't had much need for carpentry skills. He'd focused all his attention on being the best military guy he could be. That had meant working his ass off and applying for the elite Navy SEALs training.

BUD/S had been the most difficult training he'd ever survived. Once he'd made it through, he'd been deployed on a regular basis to all corners of the world, fighting wars he thought were to help people who couldn't help themselves or protect his own country from the tyranny of others.

Drake snorted. He'd learned all too soon that war wasn't always for just causes. When he'd tired of putting his life on the line for the benefit of big business, he'd said goodbye to what had been the only career he'd ever wanted.

From there, he'd worked with Stone Jacobs as a mercenary in Afghanistan, leaving just in time before the US pulled out and left Stone and the last five members of his team stranded.

Rumor had it that former SEAL, Hank Patterson, had sent a rescue team to get Jacobs and his people out.

Since Afghanistan, Drake had refused to be another hired mercenary. He'd been drifting from one low-paying job to another. Nothing seemed to fit.

When Hank Patterson had called him out of the blue, he'd been working at a small diner in the backwoods of East Texas, dissatisfied with life, unable to fit into the civilian world and ready for any change that would take him away from the diner, the small-minded residents of the town and the meddling mamas bent on matching their single daughters to the only bachelor in town with all of his original teeth.

No, thank you.

Drake had been ready to leave East Texas.

When Hank's call had come, he'd been willing to listen and even come to Montana for a one-on-one chat with his old friend and brother-in-arms.

Hank had offered Drake a job as a Brotherhood Protector, a kind of security firm providing protection, extraction and whatever else was warranted for people who needed the expertise of someone skilled in special operations.

"I'm not interested in mercenary work," Drake had said. "Been there…done that."

"It's not mercenary work," Hank had said. "It's bodyguard, rescue and protective services for real people who need specialized help. We aren't working for big corporations."

Drake had been insistent. "Not interested. Got anything else?"

Hank chuckled. "As a matter of fact, I know someone who needs carpenters for a lodge restoration project. It's good physical work, and the lodge is worth restoring."

"Sounds more my speed," Drake said.

"Come out to Montana. See what we have here and make your decision," Hank had urged.

Drake had remained firm. "I'm not going to change my mind."

"Okay. I get it. But I want you to meet the guys who work with me and get their take on what we do."

"Fair enough," Drake said. "I'd still rather pound nails. It beats slinging bullets."

"I'll put you in touch with Molly McKinnon and Parker Bailey. They are leading the effort to restore the lodge. I've sent several spec ops guys their way already. You probably know some of them or know of them."

"I'm down for some renovation work with a team

full of former spec ops guys, as long as they aren't going to try to talk me into working for your Brotherhood Protectors." He thought he might have insulted Hank. "No offense."

Hank laughed. "None taken. Whichever way you lean in the job front, you'll love Montana and the little town of Eagle Rock."

Anything would be better than the close-minded, stone-faced inhabitants of the small East Texas town he'd worked in for the past six months.

"How soon can you get here?" Hank asked. "The other four SEALs are due to start on Monday morning."

"I'll be there," Drake had assured him.

"Great. See you then," Hank ended the call.

Drake had immediately given the diner his resignation, packed up his few personal items in his furnished apartment and left Texas. He'd driven for two days, stopping only long enough to catch a couple of hours of sleep at a rest area along the way.

When he rolled to a stop in the parking lot in front of the Lucky Lady Lodge, with the Crazy Mountains as a backdrop to the old building, he already felt more at home than he had anywhere else. Maybe it was because he was tired. More likely, he felt that way because he didn't want to move again.

As he stepped down from his pickup, he shrugged off his exhaustion. He could sink his teeth into this project. It beat cleaning years of grease off the diner's floor back in Texas.

With a new sense of purpose, he passed the large roll-on-roll-off trash bin, already half-full of broken boards, crumbled sheets of drywall panels, ruined carpet and damaged furniture. He climbed the steps to the wide veranda and entered through the stately double doors of the lodge.

Six men and a woman stood in the lobby, wearing jeans and T-shirts. They had gathered around a drafting table, all looking down at what appeared to be blueprints.

The woman glanced up. "Oh, good. Drake's here."

The others straightened and turned toward Drake.

As he studied the faces, his heart filled with joy.

He knew Hank from way back at the beginning of his career as a Navy SEAL. Hank had been the experienced SEAL who'd taken him under his wing and shown him the ropes of what it was like beyond BUD/S. Clean-shaven, he had a short haircut, unlike the shaggy look he'd acquired on active duty. The man had a few more wrinkles around his green eyes, but he was the same man who'd been his mentor so many years ago.

Hank stepped forward, holding out his hand. "Morgan, I'm glad you made it. You must've driven all night to get here."

Drake took the man's hand and was pulled into a

bone-crunching hug.

"Good to see you," Hank said.

"Same," Drake said. "It's been a few years."

Hank stepped back. "I believe you know everyone here."

Drake nodded, his lips spreading into a grin.

A man with dark blond hair, blue eyes and a naturally somber expression stepped past Hank and pulled Drake into another powerful hug. "Dude, it's been too long."

"Grimm," Drake clapped his hand on the man's back. "I thought you were still on active duty."

Mike Reaper, or Grimm as he'd been aptly nicknamed, patted his leg. "Took shrapnel to my left leg. It bought me early retirement."

Drake shook his head. "Sorry to hear that."

"I'm not. I was getting too old to play with the young kids. It was time for me to move on." He nodded. "I'm looking forward to getting my hands dirty with something besides gun cleaning oil."

"Move over, Grimm. My turn." A man shoved Grimm to the side. "Bring it in, Morgan."

A black-haired man with shocking blue eyes grabbed Drake by the shoulders and crushed him in a hug. "'Bout time we worked together again," he said. "When did we last?"

"Afghanistan," Drake said when he could breathe again. He grinned at his old teammate from his last tour of duty before leaving the Navy. "We took out that Taliban terrorist who was cutting off heads for fun. How're you doing, Murdock?"

Sean Murdock stood back, smiling. "Better, now that you're here. Thought we were going to be Army puke heavy. We needed some bone frogs to level the playing field." He turned and dragged another man forward. "Remember this guy?"

Drake's brow furrowed. "Utah?"

The handsome man with the auburn hair and blue eyes smirked. "I prefer to go by Pierce. I like to think I've outgrown the Utah moniker."

Murdock laughed and pounded Utah on the back. "You'll never live down Utah. Once an uptight asshole, always an uptight asshole."

Pierce "Utah" Turner's lips pressed together. "Thanks." He held out his hand to Drake. "Good to see you under better circumstances than the last time we worked together."

Drake gripped the man's hand, truly glad to see him. "Taking mortar fire while trying to extract that Marine platoon was not one of our cleanest joint operations. You saved my life that day."

"And you returned the favor five minutes later," Utah said. "I'd call it even."

Drake glanced toward the last man he knew in the group and smiled. "Hey, Judge. You're a sight for sore eyes."

"Didn't think you'd remember me, it's been so long." Joe "Judge" Smith, former Delta Force Operative, was the old man of the group of men Drake would work with at the lodge. Like Hank, he'd influenced Drake when he was a young Navy SEAL fresh out of training. He'd been an integral part of the first joint operation of which Drake had been a part.

He'd hung back to provide cover fire for the team as they'd exited a hot zone. Judge had taken a bullet to his right forearm and had to use his left arm and hand to fire his rifle. The man hadn't missed a beat. He'd held on long enough for the entire team to reach the Black Hawk helicopters waiting at the extraction point.

When Judge hadn't been right behind them loading the aircraft, Drake had jumped out, determined to go back. He'd gone less than twenty yards when Judge had come running, dozens of Taliban soldiers on his heels.

Drake and the rest of his team had provided him cover until he'd dove aboard the helicopter. They'd lifted off under heavy fire and made it back to the Forward Operating Base without losing a single man. He'd made an impression on Drake he would never forget.

"What brings you to Montana?" Drake asked.

"Got tired of wiping the noses of baby Deltas," Judge said. "When I reached my twenty, I figured it was time to leave."

"I always wondered why they called you Judge," Drake admitted.

Judge shrugged.

Grimm laughed. "It came out of a barroom fight. Patterson didn't like the way a man was treating one of the ladies. When he told him to back off, the man asked him what he was going to do if he didn't." Grimm's lips curled. "He became the Judge, jury and executioner."

"You killed the guy?" the woman at the drafting table asked.

Judge shook his head. "No."

"He made him wish he was dead," Grimm said. "He almost got kicked out of Delta Force. If the woman he'd defended hadn't come forward to tell her side of the story, his career would've been over."

Drake glanced around at the men he'd fought with and shook his head. "Had I known we were having a reunion, I would've come sooner."

"I want each of you to know I would hire you in a heartbeat for my organization, Brotherhood Protectors, but you all have expressed your desire to fire nail guns, not Glocks. I haven't given up hope that you'll change your mind, but I respect that you want to try something different. And with that, I'll hand you over to your new bosses. Molly McKinnon and her fiancé, Parker Bailey, are from the Iron Horse Ranch." Hank waved a hand toward the man and the woman who'd remained at the drafting table. "They're the new owners of the Lucky Lady Lodge."

"For better or worse." The man took Drake's

hand. "Welcome aboard. I'm here to do the grunt work, just like you guys." He turned to the woman. "Molly is the brains behind the project."

Molly shook Drake's hand. "Glad to meet you. Now, if we could get started…"

He smiled. "Yes, ma'am."

She turned to the drawings. "We're in the demolition phase of this project. We have to clean up what was damaged in the mine explosion before we can assess structural damage," Molly said.

Parker added. "Each man has been assigned different areas to work, not too far from each other in case you run into trouble."

Molly pointed to the blueprint. "Drake, you'll take the butler's pantry and coat closet on the far side of the main dining room. The walls are cracked and crumbling. We need to get behind the drywall to see if the support beams have been compromised. Your goal today is to clear the walls on the mountainside of the rooms and any other walls showing significant damage."

Parker raised a hand. "I'll take Drake and Grimm to their locations."

Molly glanced toward the other three men. "The rest are with me. You'll find sledgehammers, battery-powered reciprocating saws, gloves and wheelbarrows staged in each of your areas. The power is off, so you'll have to use the headlamps on your safety helmets. The rooms against the mountain don't get much natural light." She handed Drake a helmet with a headlamp. "Thank you all for answering Hank's call. We needed as many hands as we could get for this project, and sometimes, people are hard to come by in small towns."

Anxious to get to work, Drake plunked his helmet on his head and followed Parker through the maze of hallways to the back of the lodge. They hadn't gone far before they had to stop and turn on their headlamps.

Parker continued, explaining what each room was as they passed doorways. He eventually came to a stop in front of a wooden door. "Grimm, this is your assigned area. Judge, yours is the next room. I'll be two doors down. If something doesn't feel right, get the hell out. We don't know exactly how much damage the explosion caused. I'd rather we err on the side of caution. The sooner we see inside the walls, the sooner we can get to work rebuilding."

"Got it." Grimm pulled on a pair of gloves, wrapped his hands around the handle of a sledge-hammer and nodded. "Nothing like a little demolition to work out all your frustrations. Let's do this."

Judge entered the next room and found what he needed to get started. Parker moved on.

Gloves on, Drake grabbed the sledgehammer and went to work knocking big holes in the plaster on the back wall. Piece by piece, he pulled away the plaster and the narrow wooden slats behind it, exposing a couple of feet of the interior beams at a time.

Plaster dust filled the air, making it more and more difficult to see. Judge found face masks in the stack of supplies and pulled one on over his mouth and nose. He'd made it through half the back wall in less than an hour. If he kept up the pace, he'd have that wall done in the next hour. The other walls in the room had only hairline fractures in the plaster. Hopefully, that was a good sign that they hadn't been damaged to the point they needed to be torn down as well.

One thing was certain; they'd have to wait until the dust settled before they could assess the status of the support beams.

The banging on the wall in the next rooms stopped for a moment.

"Can you see anything?" Grimm called out.

"Not much," Drake responded. "My headlamp is reflecting off all the dust particles."

"Same," Grimm came to stand in the doorway, wearing a mask over his mouth and nose.

"Let the dust settle for a few minutes," Parker called out.

"Have you had a chance to find a place to live?" Grimm asked.

Drake shook his head, his light swinging right then left, bouncing off the dust in the air. "I just got to town and came straight here."

"I think there's room at Mrs. Dottie Kinner's bed and breakfast where I'm staying. You can follow me there after work and ask her yourself if she's got another room available."

"Thanks." Drake glanced across the room. "I think I can see the wall again."

Grimm nodded. "Going back to my wall."

Moments later, the men were slamming their heavy sledgehammers into yet more plaster.

Drake worked on the next four feet of wall, knocking out sheetrock. He grabbed hold of a portion of the drywall and pulled hard. A large portion fell away, exposing a gap between studs that was three feet wide.

Had there been a door there at one time? He removed the rest of the plaster down to the floor and had to wait for the dust to settle in order to see the beams, much less if anything lay beyond the beams.

As the dust slowly settled, Drake's headlamp beam cut through the remaining particles to a room beyond the wall. It wasn't more than six feet by six feet square and had been carved out of the rock wall of the mountain.

He stepped between the beams into the stone-walled room. Several wooden crates littered the floor, along with a pile of what appeared to be clothing. He crossed to the crates and found them to be full of bottles of some kind of liquid. None of the bottles were labeled.

Drake suspected the bottles were moonshine and that the stash was left over from the Prohibition Era. He turned the beam of his headlamp to the pile of clothes on the floor. The cloth had a floral pattern of faded pink and yellow. Perhaps it had once been a curtain or a woman's dress.

As he neared the pile, he noticed a shoe and something that appeared to be a pole or thick stick lying beside it.

His pulse picked up, his empty belly roiling. He leaned over the pile of clothes and the shoe and froze.

The stick wasn't a stick at all. It was a bone. On the other side of it was another bone just like it.

With the handle of his sledgehammer, he moved the crate beside the pile of cloth and gasped.

On the other side of the crate, lying against the cold stone floor, lay a skull covered in a dry mummi-fied layer of skin with a few long, thin strands of hair clinging to it in scattered patches.

"Parker," Drake called out.

When the hammering continued, Drake cleared his throat and yelled. "Parker!"

All hammering ceased.

"That you, Drake?" Parker answered.

With his gaze on what he now had determined was a complete skeleton covered in a woman's dress, Drake said, "You need to come see this."

# CHAPTER 2

After Deputy Cassie Douglas had issued Drake Morgan a warning to watch his speed around Eagle Rock, she'd driven to the sheriff's office well past her shift's end.

The night had been long and uneventful, making it feel even longer than the over nine hours she'd put in from eleven o'clock the previous night to almost nine that morning.

"You're late," Sheriff Barron said as she entered the office.

"Had a traffic stop on my way in."

"Anything interesting?" the sheriff asked without looking up from his computer screen.

Yeah. Drake Morgan had been interesting. New to town. Black hair, blue eyes, and at least a foot taller than Cassie, with impossibly broad shoulders and a tight ass. "Just the usual. In a hurry to get somewhere."

"Guess he didn't get where he was going on time." Sheriff Barron chose that moment to glance up. "Give you any trouble?"

"No," she said. Except for the way her stomach fluttered when he'd given her a crooked smile and thanked her for giving him a warning.

The man had been ruggedly handsome in an unassuming way. She was human and female, and her body had reacted to him more than she would ever admit. Not that she'd act on any attraction. The frisk had been necessary to ensure her own safety. She'd learned early on in her short career as a sheriff's deputy that she should never turn her back to a man or woman until she knew for certain that person was unarmed. Even then, she didn't turn her back.

"Ticket?" the sheriff asked.

Cassie shook her head. "Warning. He didn't have any outstanding warrants. He cooperated and didn't get angry, even when I frisked him."

The sheriff grinned. "I'll bet."

She frowned. "He had a gun in his glove box. I wasn't taking any chances. The man could've been hiding another gun on his person."

Still smiling, Sheriff Barron held up his hands. "I'm not judging. A lone female on duty has to do what she has to do to stay safe."

"Damn right," she said, her lips pressing together. She glanced around. "Did Wells make it in?"

The sheriff shook his head. "His mother fell last night. He's at the hospital in Bozeman with her. Guthrie took his shift. She answered a call out at the Miller's place. Should be back in town within the next hour."

Cassie snorted. "Fat chance. Ms. Georgia Miller will keep her for more than an hour, looking over every inch of her two acres while regaling her with stories of her past as a Vegas call girl."

Sheriff Barron laughed. "You're right. The exact reason I chose to send Guthrie. She's got more patience than I do."

"I believe Guthrie has the mom gene."

"How so?" the sheriff asked.

Cassie pulled up a chair at a desk and fired up the computer. "It's the genetic predisposition to ignore certain stimuli, like a crying baby, children arguing among each other…you know, a typical day in the paradise of raising a family."

"I take it you're not all that into family," the sheriff said.

"I wouldn't mind grown children, but I'd have to get them past those awkward newborn to twenty-five stages."

The sheriff pushed to his feet. "I need to make a run to the gym. My heart doctor told me I either had to work out or die."

"Nothing like being blunt," Cassie said

He glanced at his desk, a frown pulling his brow low. "I've got so much to do…" The sheriff shook his head and started to resume his seat. "I might just skip the workout."

"Seriously, tell me what I can do for you." Cassie grinned. "You're going to be gone…what…an hour? Maybe two?"

The sheriff grimaced. "I'm almost certain I can't do more than an hour of any kind of exercise. I'll be back in an hour, no more." He pushed to his feet. "You sure you'll be okay for another hour?"

She nodded. "I'm always too wound up to sleep after coming off the graveyard shift. I might as well catch up on my paperwork."

Sheriff Barron grabbed a gym bag from beneath his desk and gave her a lopsided grin. "Then either I'll be back soon, or Guthrie will, and you can go home to bed."

"Take your time." Cassie glanced around the office. "Where's Marnie?"

"She's telecommuting," the sheriff said. "She can handle dispatch from home."

"I have no doubt about that," Cassie said. "That woman could juggle knives and talk a jumper off the ledge at the same time."

He nodded. "Just lock up if you need to leave before I get back."

"I should still be here. I want to do some more research."

The sheriff's gaze softened. "Making any progress on finding your friend?"

Cassie sighed. "Not really. You'd think that after four months, we'd have found something. Anything."

"And yet, there's been nothing." The sheriff shook his head. "No new leads?"

Cassie shook her head, her lips tightening. "I still think it's her ex-boyfriend who's done something with her."

"The detective in Los Angeles questioned him. He was at work when she disappeared. His alibi is airtight."

"Then he paid someone to do his dirty work," Cassie said. "He was an abusive bastard. I tried to get Penny to leave him. Every time she said she would, he'd start acting right again and apologize for his treatment of her."

"It's a vicious cycle. The abused woman tends to think she's the one at fault," the sheriff said.

Cassie nodded and frowned. "You're not getting to the gym by standing here, talking to me. I won't have Doc Adams chewing me out for delaying you from the lifestyle he's prescribed for you." She grinned. "Don't worry. I'll stick around and answer anything that comes up."

The sheriff drew in a deep breath and let it out. "Okay. I'm going." He pushed through the door and paused on the threshold. "If anything comes up, I can be here in less than ten minutes."

Cassie chuckled. "This is Eagle Rock, Montana. Since the James McKinnon abduction case was solved, we've had a dry spell of crime." Cassie laughed. "Not that I'm complaining. We're lucky to get one speeder every other day."

"And you've met your quota for the next two days." Sheriff Barron nodded. "Yeah. Yeah. I'm outta here."

Finally, the sheriff made it through the door and out to his service vehicle.

Cassie shook her head. Barron was a good man who did a lot for the community he served. They were lucky to have a man with such solid values and a desire to help others.

Now, if only she could find Penny and bring her home.

Cassie went online to the National Missing and Unidentified Persons database, hoping for any updates that might give her a lead to follow in Penny's disappearance.

She suspected Penny's ex because of his track record as an abuser.

Penny's car hadn't been found. For all Cassie knew, Penny and her car could have been driven off a cliff into the ocean or into a lake where no one would find her or the car for decades.

Deep down, Cassie hoped to find Penny someday,

alive and maybe held captive, not dead and buried. The odds of finding a missing person after more than forty-eight hours were slim. Four months had passed with no leads, no sightings and no sign of her car or her on any video surveillance cameras or in any airports, car lots or parking garages. It was as if Penny had disappeared off the face of the earth.

"No," Cassie said and searched even harder. She wouldn't give up.

Deep in the NamUs database, Cassie jumped when the phone on the sheriff's desk rang.

She leaped to her feet and answered. "Deputy Douglas."

"Cassie," Marnie's voice sounded in her ear, curt and anxious. "Is the sheriff around? He's not answering his cell phone."

"He's gone to the gym," Cassie said. "What do you need?"

"Got a DB at the Lucky Lady Lodge."

"Dead body?" Cassie asked.

"Yes," the dispatcher confirmed. "They found it in a hidden room in the lodge. Based on the clothing and size of the bones, Molly McKinnon and Parker Bailey suspect it's a female. I can send someone over to the gym to get the sheriff."

Cassie's heart sank to the pit of her belly. Female. Could it be Penny? She tamped down the bile rising in her throat. No. It wasn't Penny. She had to believe that. "Get the sheriff from the gym," Cassie said. "In the meantime, I'll head to the lodge and at least secure the site."

"Will you be okay?" Marnie asked. "Some people get all crazy after seeing a dead body. This will be your first."

"Don't worry about me. I'll be fine," Cassie said, poking her thumb toward her chest even though Marnie couldn't see her. Since she'd quit law school to come back to Eagle Rock to join the sheriff's department, there hadn't been a whole lot of dead bodies to see. She'd hoped that coming home would put her in a more advantageous position to chase down clues than at a university hundreds of miles away from her hometown.

Being in Eagle Rock hadn't made finding Penny any easier. She was still missing, and Cassie was no closer to finding her than when she'd first come back to town. She couldn't help but think she'd thrown away her education to settle for the position and pay of a deputy in the sheriff's department. And all for nothing.

Still, Cassie wouldn't give up. Penny's body hadn't been found. The body at the lodge wasn't Penny. The fact that they hadn't found Penny's body was a reason for hope. She wanted to find her friend. Alive.

"I'll be there in ten minutes," Cassie said.

"Roger. I'll get hold of the state crime lab," Marnie said, ending the call.

Cassie would be lucky to get to the Lucky Lady

Lodge before the sheriff. She knew that as soon as he heard about the bones, he'd be out there in a flash.

All the more reason for her to hurry.

She gathered her pen and pad, slung her bullet-proof vest over her shoulders and passed through the door, pausing long enough to lock it.

Moments later, she was in her SUV, shooting northwest through town, heading for the lodge.

And here she'd thought being a deputy was getting downright boring, sitting around, waiting for something to happen, for a lead to surface or for pigs to fly.

As she pulled in front of the lodge, she was met by a handful of men and one female, covered in a thick layer of white dust.

She dropped down from the SUV and hurried toward the woman she barely recognized beneath the dust. The gentle smile, exposing white teeth, helped Cassie identify the female as Molly McKinnon, her lifelong friend.

The two women had grown up together in Eagle Rock. Cassie, Dezi, Gabbie, Liza, Bella and Penny had been inseparable...until they'd split up to go to college. Penny had lasted a semester before following her college boyfriend from Missoula to LA. He'd been convinced he was God's gift to the film industry and needed to be closer to the action to land parts.

Molly rubbed her hands on her dirty jeans and then held them out. "Cassie, I'm so glad you came."

Cassie took her hands and squeezed them gently. "What's this about a body?"

Molly turned toward the back of the lodge, leading the way down a maze of corridors with a flashlight. "One minute, I had everything I needed for an afternoon of demo. We were making good progress until one of my guys knocked down a wall leading into what we suspect was a hidey-hole used back in Prohibition days. Anyway, Drake poked around at what was left in the hidden room and came up with… Well, you'll see." Molly crossed the room, stopped short of the back wall and pointed the flashlight into the cell beyond. "She's in there."

"Are you sure it's female?" Cassie asked.

Molly snorted softly behind Cassie. "I don't know a whole lot of guys who wear dresses or high heels. At least not in these parts. Here, you'll need this." She handed the flashlight to Cassie.

Moving past Molly, Cassie held her breath and entered the stone cell carved out of the mountainside.

The body was nothing more than bones with mummified skin stretched over it. It had to have been there a long time for the skin to mummify. The dress was nothing Penny would have worn. The pattern was too floral and old-fashioned.

Definitely not Penny. Some of the tension leached out of Cassie's body.

Without touching the body, clothing or anything

else, Cassie took pictures with her cell phone and bent low, looking for anything that might help them identify the woman.

Cassie's heart contracted for a split second. Then she shook her head and drew in a deep breath. It wasn't Penny. This body had been here a long time. Penny had only been missing for four months. It took longer for a body to reach this level of mummification, didn't it?

The body had decomposed to the point it had mummified in the dry, cool confines of the hidden stone room. A few strands of hair clung to the withered scalp. The dust created in the demolition of the wall made it impossible to determine what color the hair had been. Even though the dress was covered in a thin layer of dust, she could see the pink and lilac flowers beneath it. She looked closer. Was that a stain in the fabric?

"Hellooo!" a voice shouted from somewhere else in the Lucky Lady Lodge.

Cassie stepped through the wall joists. "That will be the sheriff."

"I'll get him," Parker said and dashed out of the room, coming back a minute later with the sheriff in tow.

"I leave you alone in the office for a few short minutes, and you stir up trouble. Thankfully, I had just finished my workout." The sheriff shook his head, a mock frown pulling his eyebrows together. "What's this about a body?"

Cassie tipped her head toward the crumbled wall and the hidden room beyond. "Appears to be a female, and based on the level of decomposition, she's been there a long time."

The sheriff stepped through the gap and studied the remains. "Talk about skeletons in the proverbial closet," he murmured. "We'll have to get the medical examiner and state crime lab to put their heads together. We'll need to know an approximate date and time of death." He stepped out of the hidden room and stopped in front of Molly. "The demo and reconstruction of this room will have to go on hold until the state crime lab has collected the evidence and the body is moved."

Molly nodded. "What about the rest of the building? Can we continue work in the other rooms?"

"I don't see why not." The sheriff's lips twisted. "You could uncover more bodies. Might as well get them all out into the open."

Molly shivered. "I wonder if she was dead or alive when she was sealed into that room."

The sheriff shook his head. "Hopefully, the ME will be able to tell us more about her. As soon as we get an approximate timeframe for how long she's been dead, we can look through the missing persons database. Until then, we'll have to wait."

Molly stepped closer to Parker.

He slipped his arm around her. "We'll work on another area until then. We hope to have the renovations complete by this fall. To do that, we have to keep moving."

The sheriff nodded. "I don't see any reason you can't demo other areas. Once the crime lab does its thing, you can continue with this room as well."

Molly and Parker led the sheriff out of the room, discussing the plans for the lodge. The other men followed, except one.

Drake Morgan.

Cassie shined the flashlight once more into the hidden room where a woman lay forgotten for who knew how long. Her chest tightened. How lonely and sad.

Footsteps sounded behind her.

"You were the one who found her," she said.

Drake came to stand beside her. "Yes, ma'am."

"Please, don't call me ma'am," she said automatically. "My name is Cassie."

"Yes, ma'am," he said. "I mean, Cassie." He tipped his chin toward the body. "Any idea who she might be?"

Cassie shook her head. "I've lived in Eagle Rock most of my life. I have no idea. I'm sure there have been cases of missing women over the years. We just need a timeframe to work with to narrow it down."

"And if there's any history on work done on the lodge, that might help you narrow it down even more." His gaze and his headlamp remained trained on the hidden room. "Whoever left her there had the skills to put up walls to cover the entrance to that room."

Cassie nodded. "I'll dig into the history of the lodge. Maybe Molly will have the records of construction efforts. The previous owners had a fundraiser event to raise money for renovations."

"Doesn't look like they made any progress," Drake commented.

"They didn't. I don't believe they ever intended to renovate the lodge. They only wanted the money." Cassie's lips pressed together. "That event was the night of the explosion in the mine."

"I'm glad the McKinnons are restoring the lodge. It has good bones—" He grimaced. "Sorry, a good foundation."

"The state historical society thinks it's worth saving. And when Molly and Parker get it up and running, it will bring in tourists, which will help other businesses in this area." She turned. "So, this was the job you were trying to get to when I pulled you over."

He nodded.

"I'd apologize for slowing you down, but—"

Drake held up his hand. "You did your job. I was speeding and deserved a ticket. Thank you for sparing my driving record. I promise to keep within the speed limit unless it's an emergency."

She gave him a tentative smile and turned to leave the room.

Drake followed.

"How long will you be in this area?" she asked.

"Depends on the work. We'll be here as long as it takes to get the Lucky Lady Lodge put back together."

"How long will that be?"

"At the least until fall. Longer, if the job takes longer."

"And after that?" She was getting too personal, but she wanted to know and couldn't help asking.

He shrugged. "I have other options."

Most likely, those options would take him away from Eagle Rock.

Cassie wasn't sure why that bothered her. She barely knew the man.

They followed the sound of voices. Before Cassie could enter what had once been the grand ballroom, Drake touched her arm.

"Cassie."

She stopped and looked up into his shadowed face, the headlamp shining down into her eyes. She blinked.

"Sorry." Drake pulled off the helmet. "I'm new in town and don't know many people. Would you consider having dinner with me?" His brow wrinkled. "If that's too much too soon, how about a cup of coffee or a beer?"

She stared up at him for a long moment. "I can't do coffee, and I'll likely be asleep through dinner, but I wouldn't mind meeting you for a beer later tonight if you're still up. I just pulled a graveyard shift, and I'll be sleeping the rest of the day to catch up."

He smiled. "That works. I'm working here the rest of the day and need time to locate lodging and get settled. How's nine o'clock sound?"

Cassie nodded. "I can make nine. But this is not a date. I'll buy my own beer. I can't have anyone accusing me of favoritism."

Drake grinned. "Just sharing a friendly beer and conversation. That's all I'm asking."

"Okay, then." She gave a curt nod. "I'll see you at nine at the Blue Moose Tavern."

Her knees shook a little, and her heart raced as Cassie caught up with the sheriff outside the lodge. "I'm headed out. I'd like to be informed about our Jane Doe, should the ME come up with anything anytime soon."

The sheriff nodded. "Will do. Now, go get some rest. You're off for a couple of days, right? Then you're on the day shift?"

She nodded. "I am. But I might come into the office to use the computers."

Sheriff Barron shook his head. "Don't you ever take a break?"

Cassie shrugged. "I do. You just don't see it because I'm out at the ranch."

"You used to run barrels when you were a kid," the sheriff said. "What happened with that?"

Her lips pressed together. "I grew up."

"Seems like ever since you went off to college, you haven't been the same happy-go-lucky, freckle-faced kid."

Cassie raised a hand to her nose and looked around for Drake. Thankfully, he'd followed Molly into another room. "I still have the freckles."

"Sure miss your folks. Your mama always made a point to stop by the office with zucchini bread or cookies. I was sad to hear of their accident down in Lake Tahoe." He stopped beside Cassie's service vehicle. "I'm glad you have your brother to help on the ranch. You two managing all right?"

Cassie nodded, swallowing hard on the lump in her throat. The loss of her parents in a multi-car pileup on the way through Salt Lake City on their first vacation in years had been a blow she didn't think she'd ever overcome.

She'd been in law school when the news of her parents' deaths had reached her. Her brother had driven all the way from their ranch near Eagle Rock to Missoula, where Cassie had been studying for end-of-semester exams in her apartment. When her brother had knocked on the door, she'd seen the grief in his red-rimmed eyes and the lines etched beside his eyes and mouth.

He'd insisted she stay in school through exams

and let him handle all the arrangements to get their parents' remains back to Montana.

She'd taken her tests in a daze. Then in the middle of test week, she'd gotten a phone call from Penny's mother. The woman had been beside herself. Penny had called to say she'd left LA and would be home in two days. Five days passed. Penny still hadn't arrived home and wasn't answering her cell phone.

Cassie had called Sheriff Barron. He'd contacted the LA Police department and placed Penny on the NamUs database.

How Cassie had passed her test, she wasn't sure. At the end of that semester, she'd left school and come home to Eagle Rock and the Double D Ranch with no intention of returning any time soon. She'd told the registrar she needed to take a leave of absence while she sorted through her parents' estate.

She wasn't sure she'd ever return to law school. After the funeral, she'd taken a job at the sheriff's office, hoping to help others while searching for her friend Penny. Having lost her parents, she realized it was just her and her brother Richard. And her friends. They were her bonus siblings. She wanted to continue to be a part of their lives.

Penny had been one of her close friends. Cassie, Molly, Dizi, Liza and Bella had drinks once a week to brainstorm more possibilities of where Penny might be.

Four months had passed since Penny had disappeared, and they were no closer to finding her. Cassie felt like she'd failed her sister.

"We're doing fine," she told the sheriff. "Richard takes care of the ranch operations. I help whenever he needs me." Which was often. Between Richard and their two ranch hands, who had been working at the Double D for as long as Cassie could remember, there was always more work than the three men could handle.

Cassie helped haul hay, mend fences, muck stalls, feed horses, cattle, pigs and chickens. She didn't have time to barrel race between working on the ranch and her work with the sheriff's department.

She climbed into her vehicle, waved at the sheriff and drove away from the lodge. Her thoughts went to the woman in the hidden room and the man who'd found her.

Butterflies fluttered against the empty wall of her stomach. She would meet Drake at the tavern that night. It would be her first date in over a year.

Cassie shook her head. "It's not a date," she said aloud. "We're just sharing conversation over a couple of beers." She wasn't sure she was ready to start dating again.

Her last relationship had been with a man who had wanted her to fit his idea of perfection. She'd fallen into the trap of trying to please him without realizing it, sacrificing her own needs and desires to make him happy. In the process, she'd made herself unhappy, having lost who she was and what she wanted out of life. Her grades had suffered, and she'd begun questioning her chosen career path.

When he'd asked her to change her hair color from brown to blond, it had been the final straw that broke the camel's back. She'd asked him what he *did* like about her. Everything he'd named had been something she'd changed about herself to make him happy.

She'd ended the relationship and focused on her studies, learning how to make herself happy alone.

Maybe she shouldn't go out with Drake. She'd finally reached a point in her life where she was comfortable in her own skin. Why complicate things?

Because she longed for more. The touch of a strong but gentle hand. Someone to hang out with.

Sex.

"That's what vibrators are for," she muttered and turned up the air conditioner on her vehicle, aiming the vent at her face that had suddenly flushed with heat.

The heat spread through her body and pooled low in her belly. She was in the prime of her sexual life. It was natural to want intimacy. She didn't have to give up her independence to make love with someone.

Not that she planned to make love with Drake. Conversation over a beer. That was all.

Sigh.

Maybe they could move beyond just talk on their next non-date.

In the meantime, she had to grab a few hours of sleep, or she'd be dragging her ass to the Blue Moose Tavern later that night. Not a good first impression for a first non-date.

Cassie lifted her chin. Then again, she wasn't out to please anyone but herself.

Her inner self reminded her that she appreciated a healthy sex life with a human partner, not a battery-powered substitute.

Part of attracting a partner was to be at least somewhat attractive.

Cassie glanced at her reflection in the rearview mirror and almost missed the turn for the ranch. Damn. Dark circles marred the skin beneath bloodshot eyes.

Sleep. She needed sleep.

And how was she supposed to do that when there was a case to solve, a friend to find and a sexy stranger to meet later that evening?

# CHAPTER 3

DRAKE SPENT the rest of the day breaking through the plaster of another room, dreading what he might find. Thankfully, he uncovered studs and beams, not more mummified bodies.

By the end of the day, his hair, skin and clothing were thick with plaster dust.

He met the other men and Molly outside the front of the lodge at five o'clock ready for a shower, food and a place to stash his stuff.

Molly grinned, her teeth the only clean place on her face. "My brothers wanted to invite all of you out to the Iron Horse Ranch for supper."

As one, the men groaned, Drake included.

Molly laughed. "I told him we'd do that on the weekend when we're not all so tired and covered in dust. Besides, I know some of you are still settling into your digs. Drake, if you can't find lodging in town, we can put you up at the ranch until you can."

"Thanks," Drake said. "I'm going to see if the bed and breakfast where Grimm is staying has another room."

Molly nodded. "You'll like Ms. Dottie. She's a character and runs a quaint and clean establishment. The offer's open if she's full up."

Drake nodded. "I'll keep that in mind."

"Thank you all for a successful, if eventful, day," Molly said. "We made a good start on the demo. I have a plumber scheduled to check for water leaks tomorrow. Hopefully, we can get some water running for us to rinse off before we leave tomorrow."

"That would be nice," Murdock said.

"See you all here tomorrow morning. Get some rest."

Molly and Parker left in a black dual-axel pickup with the ranch logo emblazoned in gold on the doors.

Judge clapped his hands together, creating a small cloud of dust. "Meet for dinner at the Blue Moose Tavern in an hour?"

"I'm in," Utah said.

"Me, too," Grimm seconded.

Murdock nodded. "I'll be there."

"I'll be there as soon as I secure lodging," Drake said.

"I'm at the same B&B as Grimm," Murdock said. "I'm pretty sure the room beside me is vacant. Hopefully, Ms. Dottie hasn't filled it."

"Only one way to find out." Grimm slung his dust-covered arm over Drake's shoulder. "Let's hope she lets us through the door like this."

Murdock chuckled. "She might make us strip in the laundry room. She reminds me of my grandmother. We'd come in from playing in the mud, and she'd make us strip to our skivvies in the mud room before we took another step inside the house."

"Ms. Dottie's place...Ms. Dottie's rules," Grimm said. "See the rest of you at the Tavern."

Each man headed for his own truck.

Drake slipped behind the wheel, regretting the amount of dust he'd leave behind. He'd need a change of clothing each day if the work continued to be as dusty as the first day on the job.

He followed Grimm and Murdock to the bed and breakfast on a side road off Main Street. They parked their trucks curbside. Drake grabbed his duffel bag and climbed the steps to the bed and breakfast behind the other two men.

A thin, older woman, dressed in polyester slacks and a floral blouse, met them at the door. "Oh, my." She pressed a hand to her mouth. "You can't come in like that. You'll have to go around the back and come in through the mud room where the washing machines are. Strip down, and leave your clothing there. I'll wash everything and have it back to your rooms by morning. You can find towels in the cabinet above the washer." She waved the men away from the front door. "Go on."

"I take it you're Ms. Dottie?" Drake said with a grin.

She nodded. "I am. Been Ms. Dottie all my life."

"I'm not a guest at your establishment," he said. "But if you have a room, I'd like to be."

"Shoo," she said, waving him toward the steps. "Of course, I have a room. Now, go before you leave dust all over the porch." She grabbed a broom and swept after them.

Murdock chuckled as he rounded the building between Drake and Grimm. "Just like Grandma."

"At least she has towels in the laundry room," Grimm said. "I wouldn't want to assault her sensibilities parading around in my boxer briefs."

Drake laughed. "At least you have boxer briefs."

Grimm shot a narrow-eyed glance toward Drake. "Commando?"

Drake grinned. "I might have to reevaluate my stance on briefs while I'm here at the B&B."

Murdock snorted. "Please."

The men entered through the back door into a large laundry room with two washers, two dryers, a wall of cabinets and a long countertop for folding.

The military had banished any modesty the men might have had upon entry. They stripped down to their briefs, or in Drake's case to his bare ass, wrapped towels around their waists and marched out of the laundry room, down a narrow hallway and into the front living area.

Murdock and Grimm waved to Drake. "See you in a few.

Ms. Dottie stepped out of a small office carrying a key. "Top of the stairs, take a left; your room is the second door on the right. We can settle up when you're decent."

He took the key from her hand. "Thank you, Ms. Dottie."

"You're welcome. Now, go." She wrinkled her nose. "You smell." Then she winked, turned and chuckled all the way through a dining area into the kitchen.

Drake hurried up the stairs and into the designated room, happy to find a queen-sized bed, dresser and a door leading into his own bathroom. Ten minutes later, he'd scrubbed the dust from his hair and every inch of his body, leaving his skin squeaky clean. He could swear he was at least five pounds lighter without all the dust.

After rinsing the tub clean, he combed his hair, ran a razor over his two-day-old beard and dressed in clean jeans and a black T-shirt. Drake pulled on his boots and belt, stuffed his wallet into his back pocket and left his room in search of his hostess.

He found her seated in a rose-pink wing-backed

chair with a light shining over her shoulder as she twisted a crochet hook through thick lemon-yellow yarn, already forming half a throw blanket.

"I heard you had a helluva welcome to our supposedly quiet little town." Her fingers moved swiftly, in and out of loops.

"It was an interesting day," he hedged. How much did the old woman know about what they'd found in the hidden room at the lodge?

"Oh, I know you found a body in one of the little hidden rooms they'd carved out of the side of the mountain to hide their moonshine in during Prohibition." She glanced up without missing a stroke with her crochet hook. "Female and has been there a while." She canted her head to one side. "Did I leave out anything?"

He shook his head. "No, ma'am."

"The dispatcher, Marnie, is my goddaughter," she said with a smug smile.

"Then you know as much as I do."

"The six-million-dollar question is who was she and why was she in that room?"

"That's two questions," a voice said from the staircase. Grimm smiled. "How are you this evening, Ms. Dottie."

"Just dandy," she said. "Glad to know you folks are working on the Lucky Lady. She deserves to be restored to her stately glory. I remember going there when I was a girl. People came from Bozeman,

Billings, Helena and even Idaho, Wyoming and Utah just to stay there. It was quite beautiful back in the day."

"We hope to be here throughout the restoration," Grimm said. "As long as we don't keep finding bodies behind the walls, we should make good progress."

"Good." She glanced up at Drake, stated an amount for the rent, and said, "You can pay me when you get the chance. If I can't trust a Navy SEAL, I don't know who I can trust."

Drake's lips quirked on the corners. "Marnie?"

"No, I heard that from Sadie McClain, Hank Patterson's wife. I ran into her at the grocery store this afternoon. She said you were the last of the five men Hank found for the lodge work." Ms. Dottie's gaze ran the length of Drake, then Grimm, and finally, Murdock as he joined them in the great room. "He picked a fine, strapping group of men for the job. I'd offer you dinner, but I bet you'd rather have a steak at the Blue Moose Tavern and a pint or two of beer. I'd go with you, but I get up at four-thirty to start breakfast for my guests. I can't be staying up past eight or nine o'clock."

"Do you want us to bring something back for you?" Drake asked.

"No. I have everything I need right here. You three go on before they run out of the good cuts they get from the beef produced at the White Oak Ranch. Hank and Sadie know how to raise fine beef. Who'd have thought the mega-movie star, Sadie McClain, would have a head for ranching."

Drake knew Hank had married the famous movie star. Word traveled fast in the ranks of the Navy SEALs.

Ms. Dottie chuckled. "They didn't know little Miss Sadie when she ran around town in her toddler-sized cowboy boots and a diaper like we all did as children. She was the cutest kid, with white-blond hair and the prettiest blue eyes..." She frowned. "But don't stand around listening to an old woman rambling."

As they stepped out onto the porch, Grimm asked, "Walk or drive?"

"It's only a couple of blocks," Murdock said. "Let's walk."

Drake fell in step with Grimm and Murdock, glad to be among men who spoke his language. Men who'd been through what he'd been through and had lived to tell about it. These men were warriors like him. They'd fought battles, been under fire and so close to death so many times, they'd stopped counting.

Like him, they were now navigating the strange waters of civilian life, alongside men and women who'd never been in a battle, never had bullets and mortars fire at them. Their biggest concern wasn't whether they would live to the end of the day or die a painful death when shrapnel ripped through their bodies.

No, they were concerned about getting their kids to baseball practice, or how Little Johnny was doing on his standardized aptitude tests and what shows to watch that night sitting in their comfortable homes with popcorn and the family pet lying on the floor beside them.

He'd missed his brothers in arms more than he'd thought he would and was glad he was back among them. Hank had done him a favor by inviting him to Montana with the promise of work that was more fulfilling than scraping dried gum from the underside of dining tables.

The Blue Moose Tavern was hopping on a Monday night, with cars and trucks filling the parking lot and music blaring through the open door.

Grimm led the way inside, where they were greeted by a young brunette teenage girl with pretty brown eyes and a nice smile. "How many?" she asked.

"We're meeting two others," Grimm started and stopped. "There they are, and they already have a table." As they walked away from the hostess, Grimm leaned toward Murdock. "Don't even think it. That girl is jailbait."

"You think?" Murdock shot a glance over his shoulder. "I would've guessed her to be at least twenty-one. She works in a bar."

"This place is a bar and a restaurant. Families

come to eat here." Grimm waved a hand, the gesture encompassing the crowded room.

Drake studied the patrons. Several families filled tables alongside groups of men in dusty jeans. Cowboys, fresh off the range, looking for a cool beer with friends to discuss the cattle market or the best fishing streams in the state.

Judge and Utah already sipped on tall glasses of beer while staring at the menu. Judge glanced up and nodded toward the men as they gathered around the table and claimed seats. "About time you two arrived. We were about to order without you."

Utah and Judge handed over their menus.

Drake leaned over to read through the one in front of Grimm. His gaze stopped at steak.

A pretty young woman with blond hair and blue eyes stopped beside Drake. "Hi, I'm Abby; I'll be your server. What can I get you to drink?"

The men ordered beer, and the waitress disappeared before they could place their food orders.

When she returned with the three beers, she set them on the table and pulled a pad from her pocket. "Are you ready to order?"

"Yes," Judge answered. "Ribeye, medium-rare, loaded baked potato and a house salad, ranch dressing."

"I'll have the same," Utah said.

"Make mine the same, only just butter on the potato," Drake said.

"I'll have a burger and fries," Grimm said.

"Same," Murdock said. "And before you go, we have a bet going on the hostess. I say she's twenty. These yahoos say she's a teenager."

The blonde grinned. "You lose. She's seventeen."

"Shoot," Murdock snapped his fingers. "I'd pegged you as seventeen. Don't tell me... You turned sixteen last month, and this is your first job."

She slipped the pad into her apron pocket. "Wrong again. I'll be twenty-one in two weeks, and I've been here for the past four years part-time while I was in high school and now college."

"I didn't know they had a college in Eagle Rock," Grimm said.

"They don't," Abby said. "I'm taking online classes and will finish school next semester at the University of Montana in Missoula."

"What are you studying?" Judge asked.

"Forensic science," she said. "I want to work with the state crime lab."

"Admirable," Murdock said.

"I'll get your orders to the kitchen. Let me know if you need refills on those drinks." Abby turned and hurried away.

"Steady, boy," Grimm murmured beside Murdock.

Murdock's lips pressed together. "Relax. She's too young. I like a woman who's established, knows what she wants and isn't afraid to go for it. Take the pretty deputy who came out to the lodge today. She's more my speed."

Drake's hand tightened around his glass. He schooled his face into what he hoped would project indifference. Inside, he wanted to shout, "Back off! The deputy is mine."

But she wasn't. He had no claim to Cassie. They were meeting, not as a date, but as two people spending time together with no expectations other than sharing a conversation over beer.

Hopefully, the guys wouldn't linger at the tavern after the meal. Drake wasn't sure where things would go with Cassie, and he didn't want his friends to know anything about their assignation. Then again, he didn't want Murdock hitting on the deputy. Then again, Cassie didn't have to be exclusive to Drake. She was her own person, making her own decisions.

At that point, Drake wished he could fast-forward his relationship with Cassie to know whether she would find him interesting enough to be more than a friend sharing a table and conversation.

It had been a long time since he'd gone on a date. He wasn't exactly sure what a single woman expected from a man. He might be old-fashioned, but he felt like he should pay for the drinks and meal if they chose to eat.

*It's not a date.*

She'd been firm about that.

"Tired?" Grimm asked, bringing Drake back to

present company, surrounded by men with whom he'd served.

Drake nodded. "A little. But breaking down walls felt good."

Murdock grinned. "Gets out all your frustrations."

"Until you stumble across a body," Judge said. "I bet that was weird."

Drake nodded. "I can't stop wondering who she was. I keep imagining the family that has gone years not knowing what happened to their loved one."

Judge nodded. "I don't know about you, but finding a body puts a damper on what we're trying to accomplish."

"Yes, it does. Thankfully, we have more walls to pound. That should help a little."

"Tearing something down and then building it up again should be cathartic," Murdock. "Kind of like what they did to us in BUD/S training. That's what we're doing with the Lucky Lady. It's not a happy place now, but maybe once we get her fixed up, she will be."

"And if we can solve the mystery about the lady in the rock room, we can put one family's minds at rest," Grimm added.

"Like releasing the bad juju from the lodge?" Murdock said. "It was creepy finding her. But you have to believe it was meant to be. She couldn't rest in peace until the secret of her disappearance was resolved."

Abby appeared weighted down by a large round tray filled with platters of food. She set the tray on a stand and distributed steaks and hamburgers where they belonged. When she was done, she slipped the tray under her arm and smiled. "Ready for another beer?"

Judge held up a hand. "Not for me."

"I'll take one," Utah said and pushed his empty glass toward Abby. Drake, Grimm and Murdock all shook their heads, not even halfway through their current drinks. Drake wouldn't order another until he met with Cassie. He wanted a clear head when he asked all the questions he had for her. He'd have to pace himself so as not to overwhelm her to the point she ran screaming from the tavern.

He was saved from further conversation as he cut into the most tender steak he'd ever sliced through with a butter knife. It practically fell apart on its way to his lips.

Drake moaned. "Wow," he said. "Ms. Dottie wasn't lying. The food here is amazing."

"I'd almost go so far as to say it's better than sex," Murdock said with a straight face. Then he grinned. "Nah, just kidding. Nothing's better than sex."

"I don't know," Drake said. "This steak comes a really close second."

The team consumed their meals in record time, washing them down with beer. When Drake was done, he pushed back his plate and groaned, "I don't think I'll need to eat again for a week."

Abby appeared with a smile. "Did you guys save room for dessert?"

They moaned as one.

"No?" Abby chuckled. "More to drink?"

Each man shook his head.

"If that's all, do you want me to split the ticket?" Abby asked.

"Yes, ma'am." Drake sure as hell couldn't afford to pay for everyone's meals. He had yet to be paid by his current job and didn't expect anything from the diner back in Texas. What savings he had, he'd vowed not to touch. Someday, he'd need that money for retirement. It wasn't too early to think that way. And as long as he was able-bodied, he'd work for the money he needed to survive.

Once the bills had been paid and the last drops were drained from their glasses, the men pushed away from the table and stood—all but Drake.

"Aren't you coming?" Grimm asked.

Drake shook his head. "You go on. I'll find my own way back. I feel like staying a little longer."

Murdock pulled out his chair. "I could stay a little longer."

"Really," Drake said. "You've got to be tired. I'm still keyed up and want to take a little more time relaxing. I don't need anyone to keep me company," he insisted.

"A man shouldn't drink alone," Judge said.

How did Drake tell his friends he didn't want them to stay without insulting them or spilling the beans about his non-date?

Grimm's eyes narrowed. "The man obviously doesn't want us to stay. The question is *why?*"

Murdock's eyes widened, and his lips spread into a grin. "Got a hot date already?"

"That has to be it. Dude, who is she?" Grimm demanded. "I figure men outnumber women ten-to-one here in Montana. How did you score a date, and you haven't even been in town a full twenty-four hours?"

Drake's cheeks heated. "It's not a date. I'm just meeting someone for a beer a little later. That's all."

"Is she a local?" Murdock asked. "I'd like to know your pickup line. Mine isn't working."

Drake shook his head. "I didn't use one. You're on your own."

Murdock's brow formed a V over his nose. "I'm crushed. You aren't going to tell us who your date is with and how you landed it." He crossed his arms over his chest. "I have half a mind to stick around and see for myself."

Grimm hooked Murdock's arm. "Come on, lover boy. Show's over. Leave the man in peace."

Murdock shook Grimm's hand free. "Okay, okay. I'm leaving. Just one last thing… If she has a sister, would you ask her if she can set me up with her?"

Grimm grabbed one of Murdock's arms, and Judge held the other. Together, they dragged Murdock out of the tavern, followed by Utah, who was too cool to be involved in a childish scuffle.

Drake would have laughed, but he was too busy looking for Cassie, hoping she wouldn't arrive too early, giving his team time to vacate the premises, inside and outside the tavern.

He glanced at this watch. Fifteen minutes until nine o'clock. His pulse picked up, and his palms actually sweated. If she didn't arrive soon, he'd be bouncing off the wall with nerves. Why did he think he'd be ready to date when he'd failed miserably at assimilating into the civilian world?

# CHAPTER 4

ABBY CAME BACK to collect the dinner dishes from the table.

"Is it possible to get a smaller table in a more secluded area?" Drake asked.

"Sure," Abby said. "Let me see what's available." A couple of minutes later, she returned. "Come with me."

She led the way to a booth with high sides in the far corner of the tavern. "This is about as secluded as it gets."

Now that he'd found the perfect spot, out of view of everyone else, Drake worried it was so out of the way that Cassie wouldn't find him.

"Abby," Drake stopped her before she got away.

"Is there something I could get for you?"

"Not yet," Drake answered. "Do you know Deputy Douglas?"

Abby's eyebrows formed a V over her nose. "Cassie Douglas?" she asked.

"Yes," Drake said with a smile.

"Sure do. Why?"

"If you see her enter the tavern, will you send her my way?"

Abby's brow smoothed with a smile. "Is she your date?"

Drake started to say no; Cassie wasn't his date. But it was easier for Abby to understand a date than to tell her their get-together was just for conversation. Anything more than conversation would be pushing things way too fast.

Over the next fifteen minutes, Drake leaned out of the booth no less than twenty times.

About the time he decided to relax and let whatever happened happen, he heard Abby say. "He's been waiting for you for the last fifteen minutes. I have you two in the booth farthest from the bar, the large family in the opposite corner and the kitchen. You shouldn't be disturbed here. What can I get you to drink?"

"I'll have a whiskey neat, please. How's your mother? I haven't seen her around town in a while."

Abby's smile faded. "She's been sick and confined to her room. Dad takes her meals to her, so I don't catch whatever she's got. I barely see her between work and studying at the library."

"I hope she feels better soon," Cassie said as she slipped onto the bench across from Drake.

"Me, too," Abby said. "I'll be right back with your drink." She started to walk away, stopped and turned to Drake. "Sorry. I meant to ask whether you're ready for something."

Drake nodded. "I'll have what she's having."

Abby nodded. "Two whiskeys neat." And she left them.

"Did you get the sleep you needed?" Drake asked.

Cassie shrugged. "Some. I didn't want a full eight hours because I have to transition to the day shift in a few days. I slept for four hours and helped out in the barn. I just had enough time to shower off the smell of horse manure before I came." She gave him a crooked smile. "Yeah. I'm not the kind of woman who primps and spends a lot of time in front of the mirror. What you see is what you get."

"I like that about you."

She snorted. "You'd be the first man who does."

Drake frowned. "I take it someone didn't appreciate you the way you deserve?"

"It's not important. I'm learning to leave the past in the past. Except when it involves a woman sealed in a hidden room. Now that's some past I want to sink my teeth into."

"Heard anything?" Drake asked.

Cassie nodded. "They took her body straight to Missoula, where the state crime lab is. They were freakishly excited about her mummified remains and promised to get right on it, even if it meant working through the night."

"Any possibility they'll have some news by morning?"

"I don't know. They'll probably start with dental records, looking for a match with the missing persons database," Cassie said. "It would be negligent for me to say they could have something by morning. They never work that fast."

"It's not like I'll be waiting around for a call from Missoula. We're just getting started on the demolition."

"How's that coming? Is there any major structural damage?"

"So far, very little. A couple of support beams were compromised closest to the explosion inside the mine. Molly had an engineer evaluate the damage. They think it could be easily shored up. It shouldn't be long before we move from demolition to reconstruction."

"I'm glad to hear that," she said with a smile.

Abby arrived with their drinks and a bowl full of chips and salsa. "Thought you might like some munchies."

"Thank you, Abby." Cassie's brow furrowed. "I thought you only worked until nine on weeknights during school."

Abby shrugged. "That was during high school. I

try to get home early on weeknights during a regular college semester, but online classes make it easy to do the work on my own time." She laughed. "Don't worry. I'm leaving now unless you want something else. And after I leave, you only have to tell the bartender what you want, and he'll be glad to help."

"You can close out our bill...to wrap up your night," Drake said.

"Bills," Cassie corrected. "We're going Dutch."

"I'll be right back." Abby left, returning shortly with their two separate bills.

Drake and Cassie both gave her cash with generous tips

Abby grinned. "Thank you. I'm saving for when I return to campus next fall. Rent prices have gone up." She squared her shoulders. "I don't want to graduate with a huge student loan debt." Abby glanced at the clock on the wall. "I need to get going. You two have a good night."

"Thank you for all you do," Cassie said.

"Thank you for believing in me and setting a great example for me to live by." Abby leaned close and hugged Cassie. When she straightened, she glanced at Drake. "Take good care of her. She's the real deal."

He nodded, not wanting to tell the young woman they weren't on a date.

Abby left them alone.

A long, awkward silence stretched between Drake and Cassie.

"I know you didn't want this to be a date, but I have to tell you...I wish it had been."

Her brow wrinkled. "Why? So we could sit here even more awkwardly than we are now?"

"That's not what I had in mind."

She lifted her chin and stared down her nose challengingly. "What would you have done differently?"

"I would've picked up the check, for one," he said.

"Which makes a woman feel obligated to give something in return, with the usual expectation being sex." She didn't give him a chance to repute. "Go on."

"We would've had dinner and drinks and explored each other's life histories."

"This will be quick." She tapped a finger to her chin and stared off into the corner. "I was born and raised in this area. I know everyone, and everyone knows me. I was a barrel racer in high school, but quit after going to college. Majored in criminal science, applied for law school and dropped out one year short of completion. I've never been married, no children but one brother. My parents died in a car crash less than a year ago, and I've only been in one semi-long-term relationship that I was glad to end. I work for the sheriff's department, mostly in a four-wheeled vehicle. Sometimes, my job requires me to saddle up on horseback."

She planted her elbow on the table, propped her chin on her fist and raised her eyebrows. "Your turn."

On the spot, he hesitated. "Wow, when you make it so blunt, it's hard to know where to start."

"Where did you grow up?" she asked.

"Texas Hill Country."

"Do you ride horses?" she asked. "That's important to me. The last guy I dated didn't. I consider that a huge strike against a potential man in my life."

Drake laughed. "I ride."

"What's your background?"

"I spent nearly fourteen years in the Navy, the last ten as a Navy SEAL, deploying to places I didn't know existed until we landed there in Black Hawks. I've been shot three times, hit with shrapnel from mortars and IEDs and I despise politics and politicians." He frowned, then smiled. "Oh, and I love dogs."

Cassie laughed. "I have a soft spot for dogs. Had one up to the time I left for college. He died of old age when I was away. I will always regret that I wasn't home with him. I also regret that I wasn't with my parents before they left on the vacation that killed them."

"I'm sorry for your losses. It had to be hard." He sighed. "My folks passed while I was deployed. I didn't get word until three weeks after they'd been interred."

"No closure." Cassie shook her head. "I feel you. Relationships?"

Drake chuckled. "I dated a few women, but none of them caught my attention long enough for me to ask them out on a second date. I just wasn't that interested."

"I'm sorry to say it, but I'm not that interesting. I live a life of service to my community, and I have obligations toward the running of the Double D Ranch. I haven't been all over the world. I have been to Mexico and Canada on short trips at spring break with some of my fellow undergraduates." She smiled. "Now that we know everything there is to know about each other, what's left?"

"I would take my date out into the country and spread a blanket in the truck bed. Then we'd lie there, staring up at the stars."

Cassie leaned back. "I don't think I've ever been taken on a date where we ended up actually staring up at the stars. I'm intrigued."

"If you're up for it, we can do it tonight," he said.

"I'm up for it if you are," Cassie said. "You're probably running on less sleep than I had."

"I can function on less sleep," he assured her.

"Give me a minute to wash my hands and use the facilities," she said, pushing to her feet. "I'll be right back."

Drake's heartbeat pounded against his ribs. He was about to take a beautiful woman out stargazing.

If he was really lucky, he might even steal a kiss. Anything else would be purely icing on the cake.

And he liked cake.

CASSIE MADE her way to the ladies' room, where she used the facility, washed her hands and stared at herself in the mirror.

"This was not supposed to be a date," she reminded herself.

*But stargazing,* her inner self said.

And if he wanted to kiss her?

*Oh, hell yeah.*

Her body heated as her blood raced through her system, making her hot to the core.

She splashed cool water on her heated cheeks and dried her hands and face before leaving the bathroom.

As she left the ladies' room, she heard loud voices from the direction opposite the barroom. She turned toward the sound to find a back emergency exit standing wide open.

The voices sounded again.

Cassie recognized Abby's voice and hurried to find out what all the commotion was about.

When she stepped out the back door, she had to step back into the building quickly to avoid being targeted.

Abby stood in front of her car, a frown marring

her smooth brow. "Move out of my way, Bryan. I'd like to go home."

The young man blocked her door with his body. "Not until you talk to me."

"We're done talking, Bryan. I broke up with you. The end. We're over. Now, move so I can go home and get some sleep. I have a test tomorrow I need to study for."

He shook his head and crossed his arms over his chest. "I'm not moving until you admit you love me."

Abby sighed. "I don't love you, Bryan. You're too possessive and jealous. I'm not yours to own, and I don't have time for jealous tantrums. Now, move."

Bryan's face darkened.

Cassie could tell the young man wasn't taking rejection well. She was just about to step through the back door when Bryan made his move.

He lunged for Abby, grabbed her arm and dragged her toward him.

Abby cried out, spun and jerked her arm free.

She ran two steps before Bryan grabbed a handful of her hair and yanked her backward.

Cassie ran forward. "Bryan Mosley, let go of Abby's hair," she called out in her most authoritative tone. At five feet two, Cassie fought to project power and strength in a commanding voice. But that voice squeaked, making her sound more pathetic than powerful.

It couldn't be helped. She'd have to get physical to make Bryan let go of Abby.

Channeling her self-defense training, she rushed Bryan, grabbed his arm and twisted it up behind his back.

He let go of the handful of Abby's hair and flung himself backward, crushing Cassie against the exterior wall of the Blue Moose Tavern and knocking the air from her lungs.

He held her there for what seemed like an eternity in which she couldn't suck in a deep lungful of air. "Let. Me. Go," she wheezed.

"Leave me alone," Bryan said through clenched teeth. "Abby is my girlfriend. She loves me. I won't let anyone else have her. She's mine."

"I don't belong to anyone, Bryan. Especially not you," Abby marched up to him. "Let go of Cassie," she said. "She's not getting any air with you crushing her. You're killing her." Abby pounded the young man's back.

Without oxygen, Abby's vision blurred, and her knees weakened. If he didn't let up soon, she'd pass out. Then what would happen to Abby?

On the verge of everything fading to black, Bryan was dragged backward, losing his grip on Cassie. She slumped to her knees, sucking in deep breaths to fill her starving lungs.

Drake stood in front of her with Bryan's arm

shoved high up between the younger man's shoulder blades. Bryan danced on his toes to ease the pain.

"Apologize to the ladies," Drake demanded.

"I didn't do anything wrong," Bryan insisted.

"You attacked them. I'd call that wrong." Drake pushed Bryan's arm even higher. "They're waiting."

"You're hurting me," Bryan cried.

"And I'll hurt you even more if you don't apologize and promise not to bother these women...ever again. Say it."

Bryan grunted, his face bright red, sweat beading on his forehead. "Okay, okay. I'm sorry."

"For what?" Drake asked.

"For bothering you," Bryan said in a rush.

"And..." Drake prompted.

"And I won't do it again."

Drake nodded toward Cassie. "I'm going to escort this man to the front of the building; I suggest you and Abby make your exit now."

"Abby's leaving now." Cassie's gaze met Abby's.

"I'm going," Abby said.

While Drake walked Bryan around the side of the tavern, Abby climbed into her vehicle. Moments later, all Cassie could see were Abby's taillights as she drove away.

Alone, Cassie straightened and brushed the dust off her clothes, glad for the air to breathe.

Then Drake rounded the corner of the tavern

without Bryan, a tight smile lifting the corners of his mouth. "Still want to see the stars?" he asked.

Cassie nodded. "Absolutely."

He grimaced. "My truck is over by the B&B if you'd care to take a stroll with me." Drake offered her his arm.

Cassie looped hers through his and walked beside him to the corner. "Stars, huh?

"Gotta be the best show in town with these big skies."

"So I've heard," Cassie smiled up into Drake's eyes, ready to take a chance on this man.

# CHAPTER 5

DRAKE HELD the door for Cassie to climb into his truck. Once he'd settled into the driver's seat, he pulled out onto Main Street. "You've lived here your whole life; where's the best place to stargaze?"

Cassie grinned. "As teens, we used to get together at the bluffs overlooking the river to watch the Perseid meteor shower." She gave him the directions and leaned back in her seat.

"A teen hangout. Hopefully, not on a school night." Drake shot a glance in her direction. "Let me guess…when you hung out here, alcohol was involved."

With a shrug, Cassie nodded. "There might have been a party or two there. It was the favorite necking site until Deputy Barron started making it a regular stop on his weekend night shift. After that, the teens rotated hangout sites to keep the sheriff's department guessing."

"Now that you're part of the sheriff's department, are you policing the fresh batch of teens?"

She nodded, a grin spreading across her face. "It helps keep the teen pregnancy rate down and breaks up the parties before anyone gets so drunk they'll fall off a cliff. The parents like it."

Drake chuckled. "I'm sure the teens aren't as appreciative."

"Not at all. But then I'm not doing this job to make friends. I want the people of my community to be safe and live long, healthy lives."

"You care about them."

"I do. So many of them are like family. Especially since I lost my folks."

"Do you have a strong support network of friends?" he asked.

She nodded. "I grew up with what we called our band of sisters. The six of us went through grade, middle and high school together. We were there for each other when we had our first crushes, first breakups, a couple of weddings, a miscarriage and divorces."

"Do all six of you still live here?"

Cassie glanced away, her sad face reflected in the window. "All but one."

"Where did she end up?"

"Los Angeles. She followed her boyfriend out to

Hollywood. He was set on becoming the next big movie star."

"And did he?"

"No. He's done a couple of commercials, but no big breakthroughs. The last I heard, he was a valet at a high-end hotel."

"And your friend?" He glanced at Cassie in time to see her grimace.

"I don't know where she is. She phoned her mother four months ago, saying she was coming home for good." Cassie stared out the front windshield. "She never made it."

"What do you mean?"

"She disappeared. I've been searching for her ever since. She's listed on the missing persons database, but nothing has come up. Even her car has disappeared. I think her boyfriend did something, but the LAPD confirmed his alibi for the night she left their apartment. He was in San Francisco that night with several friends."

"No way to trace credit cards?"

Cassie gave a humorless laugh. "We've tried everything. "I think she would've used cash. Her boyfriend was abusive. We subpoenaed her bank records. She withdrew all of her money the day before she called her mother. She was preparing to run and probably didn't want to leave a trail of credit card receipts."

Drake nodded. "Which makes it even harder to trace her."

"Exactly," Cassie said. "If she hadn't called her mother and said she was coming home, I would've suspected her of going into hiding. But she wouldn't have gotten her mother's hopes up if she hadn't planned on coming home."

"Unless she determined coming home would put her family in danger…?"

"That's a possibility," Cassie said. "But she would've found a way to tell her folks she'd changed her mind."

"Is your missing friend part of the reason you're so determined to discover the identity of the woman we found behind the wall?"

Cassie nodded. "I know how my friend Penny's mother has grieved for her daughter, praying she'd come home safe and sound. I would want to know, once and for all, what had happened to my loved one. It gives closure."

"Good point." He drove on in silence.

Cassie guided him to the spot and waited until the truck rolled to a stop and he'd shut off the engine before she smiled and asked, "What do you think?"

He pushed open his door and climbed down. Before he could round the front of the truck, Cassie was out, meeting him in front.

Drake stared out across the sky bathed in indigo, a million stars providing enough illumination he could see the bluffs, the river below and the mountains surrounding them.

"Wow," he said.

She laughed. "This place at night has always had that effect on me." Cassie leaned her back against his truck's hood and stared at the stars. "I lived in Missoula through most of the years I attended college. The city lights make it hard to see the stars. Sometimes at night, I would drive away from Missoula until the city lights faded and I could see the stars again. It reminded me of here."

As Cassie spoke, Drake panned his surroundings, the blanket of stars above, and finally, let his gaze settle on the woman beside him.

She raised her face to the heavens as if bathing in the starlight, letting its radiance wash over her.

And it did, giving her skin a blue glow that emphasized her inner radiance.

"Beautiful," she whispered.

"Yes," he agreed. "Won't your neck get sore tilted back like that?"

She straightened and rubbed the back of her neck. "A couple of lounge chairs would be nice about now."

"I don't have any lounge chairs." Drake rounded to the side of the truck, opened the back door and pulled out the sleeping bag he kept rolled up behind the seat for emergencies. "I could spread this out on the ground."

"Perfect," she said with a grin. "How about

spreading it out in the back of the truck? I'd rather not tempt the snakes to cuddle up beside us."

"Good point." Drake untied the strings, unrolled the bag, unzipped it and shook it out. He lowered the tailgate, climbed into the back of the truck and spread out the bag.

Cassie hiked her bottom up onto the tailgate and swung her legs around. "Is there room for two?"

"There is." He waited for her to settle on the sleeping bag and dropped down beside her, lacing his hands behind his head. "Better?"

"Much." She stared up at the stars. "The Perseid meteor shower is in the fall, but I can usually spot a shooting star on any given clear night. Sometimes, I'll spot the International Space Station shining brightly overhead."

Drake sighed and drank in the silence and vastness of the night. "I don't need to see meteors, space stations or the rings of Saturn. Just lying here fills me with a peace I haven't felt in a long time."

"It is nice to escape the chaos of everyday life."

"Agreed," he said. "What chaos follows you?"

"The feeling that I'm not doing enough to find my friend. Having a cold case to resolve to give a family answers. Figuring out how to help my brother manage a ranch now that we're the older generation."

"It's a heavy burden you carry," he said.

She snorted softly. "I'm sure it all sounds like first-world problems compared to the stress and lingering nightmares of battles with people shooting at you, lobbing grenades and dropping bombs on you from airplanes."

"While in the battles, it's just another day on the job. Only there's a constant sense of urgency. You have to keep moving. Your life depends on it.

"Back here, it's more about appearances, rules and restraint. We're forced to assimilate into a society that will never understand what we've lived through. Most civilians have never had a buddy blown to shreds in front of them or had one bleed out in their arms."

"No, most of us haven't experienced that," Cassie whispered.

"I was glad Hank called to ask me to come work with other men like me. The men of the team working the demo are all prior military, spec ops. We speak the same language and know things." Drake stared up at the vast blanket of stars filling the sky. It could have made him feel smaller...alone. But it didn't. With his team nearby... "It's like coming home."

Cassie scooted closer and rested her head against his shoulder.

"Cold?" he asked.

"A little," she said, pressing her body closer.

He lowered his arm, letting it curl around her.

For a long time, he lay still, looking up at the stars, barely aware of their shining glory when all he could think about was the woman whose body fit against him like a glove.

His groin tightened, and heat burned through his veins. He had to tell himself it was too soon for a lot of things. They'd only just met.

If he was lucky, he might score a kiss. But he wouldn't push for more. He sensed that the time had to be right, and she had to make the first move.

It took a strong woman to be a sheriff's deputy. Drake wouldn't want anything less. If it meant proving to her he wasn't an asshole like her last boyfriend, he'd do it. If it meant waiting until she was ready...he knew she would be worth the wait. She loved deeply and cared about the people of her community.

His arm tightened around her, then he loosened his hold, giving her freedom to move.

Cassie turned on her side and laid her hand on his chest. "What are you thinking about?"

"Kissing you." The words left his mouth before he could stop them. "But don't worry. I promise not to take advantage of you."

She pushed up onto her elbow, her brow furrowing. "Seriously? Do I have to make all the moves?" Then she leaned over him and pressed her lips to his.

The heat in his veins flared, yet he held back, wanting to give her the lead.

She pressed her lips to his for a long moment and

then leaned back, her frown deepening. "I take it you're not feeling it."

"Oh, baby, I'm feeling it, all right," he said with a laugh. "I just don't want to make any sudden moves and scare you with just how much I want to kiss you back."

Her lips curved in a sexy smile. "I don't scare easily." She lifted her chin and narrowed her eyes. "You really want to kiss me?"

He nodded, holding back with every ounce of control he could muster. "And some."

Her brow dipped. "Then what are you waiting for? A written invitation? First kisses are an experiment in compatibility. If the kiss doesn't do it for you, you might need to be just friends. After your response to my kiss…you're dangerously hovering in the friend zone."

"Is that so?" He laughed. "Challenge accepted."

Drake reached for her, cupped her cheeks in the palms of his hands and took her lips in a kiss so tender, it almost hurt him to hold back.

When Cassie opened to him, her tongue meeting his, Drake couldn't hold back another second. He rolled her onto her back and came down over her, crushing her mouth with his.

Her hands moved over his shoulders and around to his chest, inching lower to the waistband of his jeans. Knotting her fists in the jersey fabric, she tugged the shirt out and slipped her fingers beneath it to press against bare skin.

Drake's breath lodged in his lungs.

Everywhere she touched burst into flaming synapses, sending electricity shooting through his body, stoking the fire coiling in his loins. He hardened so fast that he had to adjust his jeans with one hand while leaning on the other and lengthening the kiss that only got better with each stroke of her tongue.

By the time he raised his head, he was so turned on, he was afraid he'd lose control and take their kissing experiment to the next level. He dragged in several deep breaths before he could push air past his vocal cords. "Still in the friend zone?"

Her eyes flared, catching the light from the star-studded heavens. "Nowhere near," she said, her voice husky and breathless.

"Every cell in my body is screaming for me to take you hard and fast."

Her tongue swept over her bottom lip. "Are you listening?" she whispered.

"Sweet Jesus, I can hear nothing else but the caveman pounding his chest." He leaned down, pressing his forehead to hers. "The gentleman in me is struggling to be heard. It's too soon. We need time to get to know each other."

She gripped his shirt. "Seriously? Stop listening to the gentleman inside and go with the caveman." She planted her lips on his. "That kiss…wow. It brought out the cavewoman in me."

He grinned. "Good. I didn't want to be confined to a friend zone."

Her fingers tightened in his shirt. "You're not focusing."

"I'm not?" He chuckled. "Where were we?"

"Bring back the caveman."

He shook his head. "Too soon."

Her frown deepened. "What if we get to know each other and we're back in the friend zone? We will have missed out on that wild, passionate ride with lust. Life is short. You could be hit by a bus tomorrow, and you will have missed out on what could be the best sex of your life."

"Is that so?" He kissed the tip of her nose and her right eyelid. "I like your confidence."

She growled. "You're not listening."

"I'm listening. I'm just not going to make love with you our first night under the stars."

Cassie flopped back against the sleeping bag. "You're not going to change your mind?"

He shook his head. "No. You deserve better."

"I deserve what I want," she muttered. "And up until now, I wanted you." She sat up. "If we're not going to take advantage of a sky full of stars and make mad, passionate love, you might as well take me back to my car. I need a cold shower and a good night's sleep to get over this blatant rejection."

He sat up beside her and turned her face toward him. "Can I take you out for dinner tomorrow night?"

She stared at him through slitted eyes. "Will there be stargazing afterward?"

He nodded. "If you'd like."

"Will we only be kissing?" She lifted her chin as if in challenge.

His lips curled into a bone-melting smile. "If you'd like," he said.

"What if I want more?" she demanded.

"Then I'll come prepared, unlike tonight."

Her eyes opened wide. "Is that it? You're not prepared?" She threw back her head. "Thank the Lord. I thought there was something wrong with me."

All humor left his face, and only the serious SEAL looked at her now. "Sweetheart, there is nothing wrong with you. In fact, there's everything so right with you, I can't fuck it up." He slipped out of the truck bed and stood, holding out both hands.

She eased to the end of the tailgate and let him lift her, holding her body against his as she slid slowly to the ground.

When her pelvis rubbed over his engorged staff, her eyes widened. "Are you going to be all right waiting until tomorrow?"

He nodded. "Nothing a cold shower won't cure."

"I could do something to relieve the…pressure."

She cupped the front of his jeans and squeezed gently.

Drake groaned and almost lost it then. He captured her wrist in his hand and pulled her away. "Tomorrow."

She stared up into his eyes. "Promise me something."

"Anything," he said, brushing his lips across her forehead.

She leaned into him. "Don't get hit by a bus."

# CHAPTER 6

CASSIE BARELY SLEPT THAT NIGHT, her body burning with a need she'd never experienced before. A cold shower did nothing to cool the fire, and a walk outside in the night, under the stars, only served as a reminder of what had almost happened in the back of Drake's truck.

Up before dawn, she fed the animals, mucked two stalls and led the horses out to pasture for the day. She didn't feel like eating and wasn't in the mood to talk with her brother. What would she say when he asked what was wrong?

*I'm horny as hell, and the man I'm lusting after turned me down.*

She shook her head, grabbed her keys and headed for the door.

Before she could turn the door handle, Richard appeared at the entrance, scrubbing a hand through his hair and yawning. "Leaving so early? I thought this was your day off?"

She forced herself to turn and look as normal as possible. "It is. But I want to spend some time on the computers today."

"Looking for the identity of the woman in the hidden room?" he asked.

She nodded. "I've already fed the animals and cleaned Misty and Thunder's stalls. I won't be home for dinner and will likely be late, so don't worry about me."

Richard frowned. "You were out late last night. Is there something you'd like to tell me?"

She shook her head, giving him an innocent, wide-eyed look. "No."

"Would I trust him?" he asked.

She refused to answer.

Her brother's lips twisted. "I get it. Mind your own damned business." He pulled his wallet from his back pocket, dug inside and pulled out a foil packet. "If you aren't going to give me all the details, how will I know where to look for the body?" He took her hand and pressed the condom into her palm. "At least use some protection."

"Richard!" Cassie's cheeks burned.

"I'm a guy. I know what other guys are after. Not all of them are considerate enough to protect themselves, much less the woman." He tipped his head toward the door. "If you need me to come pick you up, day or night, I'm a phone call away."

Her cheeks still burning, Cassie's eyes filled. "Thanks." Then she dove for the door and spun up gravel and dust racing out of the yard in her SUV.

She and Richard had been close as kids and teens, only drifting apart when she'd gone on to college in Missoula.

Since their parents' deaths, he'd stepped up to what he must have considered his familial responsibility of looking out for his sister.

Her heart swelled with the love she felt for her only living blood relative. If anything happened to him, she'd be alone.

Well, not quite alone. She had her sister posse and the support of her hometown. As long as she lived in Eagle Rock, someone would always be looking out for her well-being.

Awake but unfocused, she made a beeline for Al's Diner, pulling into the parking lot full of trucks and SUVs. She found a spot, parked and entered through the swinging glass door.

"Morning, Cassie," Daisy Chadwick called out from across the room. "Find a table. I'll be with you in a minute."

"I'm just here for coffee," Cassie said. "No hurry. It's my day off."

"I'll meet you at the bar. Give me a minute." The

perky blond waitress finished taking an order and hurried to deliver it to the kitchen.

Cassie slipped onto a stool at the bar next to Frank Matson. His daughter Abby leaned forward and waved. "Good morning, Cassie."

Cassie smiled. "Good morning, Abby, Mr. Matson."

Frank nodded. "Morning."

Daisy appeared in front of her with a pot full of coffee and a ceramic mug. She plunked the mug in front of Cassie and filled it to the brim. "No cream or sugar, right?"

Cassie nodded and wrapped her hands around the steaming cup. "Just coffee." She leaned over the brew and inhaled, content to wait for it to cool a bit before taking her first sip.

"Daddy," Abby said, "Cassie and her new friend, Mr. Morgan, were the ones who helped me with Bryan last night when he got belligerent."

Frank turned to Cassie. "Thank you for helping my daughter. That boy needs someone to put a bag over his head and beat him with a baseball bat."

"I wouldn't recommend that," Cassie said. "You might get a whole lot of satisfaction out of doing it, but then you'd catch some jail time for assault."

"That boy won't listen," Frank said, shaking his head. "My Abby broke up with him because he wanted to control her every move, who she talked to and even what she ate."

"You might have to get a restraining order against him," Cassie said.

Frank nodded. "Exactly. I'll set up a meeting with my attorney for later today. Can't have him cornering Abby in an alley again. He's got a screw or two loose in that head of his. No telling what he'll do. He's too much like his father. I remember when my Linda dated him back when we were all in high school. Joe pulled the same stunt. We actually got into a fistfight. He stopped bothering her after I beat the snot out of him."

"Nowadays, you'd be hauled off to jail for assault. I'll keep an eye out for Abby, but I can't be everywhere." Cassie nodded toward Abby. "Have one of the staff members at the tavern walk you to your car when you leave at night."

"I will," she said. "Something has to get through his thick skull. I want nothing to do with him."

Cassie sipped her coffee, letting the rich liquid burn down her throat, warming her belly and helping her to wake up and become fully focused on the task ahead of her.

With her first shot of caffeine, she asked, "How's your wife, Mr. Matson? I haven't seen much of her since I returned to Eagle Rock."

"She's not doing so well. You know she's got Lupus, and the doc's afraid she's slipping into dementia. They want to run more tests, but she doesn't want to leave her room."

"I'm sorry to hear that. Do you have someone sitting with her while you work?" Cassie asked.

"Not yet." Frank stared into his coffee mug. "She can still get around on her own. It's just that, sometimes, she doesn't remember things just the way they are or were. It confuses her and scares her. The only place she feels safe is in our bedroom. I have a mini-refrigerator, a loveseat and a television set up for her. We're muddling along for now."

"She doesn't even want to see me sometimes." Abby frowned. "She forgets I'm her daughter." She smiled softly. "I've been reading up on dementia and Alzheimer's as part of my microbiology class. Some diseases are genetic. Which means I could get lupus, dementia and Alzheimer's someday." Her lips pressed together. "I can only hope I have more of my father's genes in me than my mother's. He's as healthy as a horse, if a little overweight." She poked her father's belly. "We need to eat a healthier diet."

He wrapped his arm around her and gave her a brief hug. "I have to get to work. That filling station isn't going to build itself." He kissed the top of Abby's head, pushed to his feet and nodded toward Cassie. "Thanks again for looking out for my girl."

Frank Matson dropped money on the counter and left the diner.

Abby scooted over one stool closer to Cassie, moving her plate of eggs and bacon with her. "I really am worried about mental illness in my family. Mama is losing more and more of her memories every day. Daddy doesn't want to talk about it. I asked him if the doctor had researched my mother's family history to see what diseases were prevalent. He said the doctors didn't have time to go back that far."

"There might not be much history to pull from," Abby said. "Some diseases might not have been correctly diagnosed."

"Mama and Daddy never talk much about their families. The only grandparent I knew was Mama's father, but he died when I was little." She smiled. "So, I decided to do a little research of my own."

"How so?" Cassie asked.

"I bought one of those DNA tests and joined the ancestry group. I should be getting the results back in a day or two. I didn't tell my father because he's so busy and has never wanted to talk much about family." She shrugged. "It would be nice if I found some long-lost relatives. I never had siblings, aunts, uncles or cousins. You're so lucky to have a brother. When you have children, they'll get to play with their cousins." Abby sighed. "Anyway, I've been keeping it a secret, and I just had to share it with someone."

Cassie cocked an eyebrow and glanced over her coffee mug at Abby. "I take it you want me to keep it a secret?"

Abby nodded. "Please. It might mean nothing; however, until I know more, I don't want to bother my father."

Cassie nodded. "My lips are sealed."

Abby slipped off her seat. "I have to go log into my online class. Will you be at the tavern tonight with your fella?"

Cassie frowned. "He's not my fella."

"No?" Abby's brow puckered. "You two are so cute together. I could practically see the chemistry between you."

"And that's the science you're learning?" Cassie chuckled.

"Actually, studies indicate men and women are attracted to pheromones and testosterone they emit." Abby blinked. "You two must have been emitting just the right amounts. Your chemistry was off the wall. The same study also talked about the first kiss."

Cassie's chuckle stuck in her throat, and heat rose up her neck into her cheeks. "What about the first kiss?"

"It was considered a dealbreaker. If the first kiss didn't do it for one or the other, there would be no more. If it hit the right connection, there would be more." Abby tilted her head. "I bet your first kiss was all lightning bolts and fireworks."

Cassie didn't say anything, her cheeks burning as she recalled the electricity shooting through her as they'd shared their first real kiss.

Abby's grin spread across her face. "Yeah, I called it. You two had some serious chemistry. Make sure you sit at one of my tables tonight. I'll make sure you have some privacy and champagne." The young woman flitted out of the diner like a fairy sprinkling sunshine.

"She's way too perky for me," Cassie muttered.

"I know what you mean," Daisy said. "But you can't help but love her. Her mother was never as happy and outgoing and…well, you know her father. He can be a taciturn grump at his best. How did two such unhappy people produce Abby?" She shook her head, her gaze following the object of their discussion. She sighed. "Need a refill?"

Cassie put her hand over her mug. "Not in here. But I'd love one to go. It's going to be a long day at the computer."

Daisy pulled a paper cup from the cabinet behind her, filled it with coffee and fit a cap over the top. "That should hold you until lunchtime. Want me to put in an order for a club sandwich to be delivered to the sheriff's office at noon?"

"That would be awesome." For a moment, Cassie thought about picking up two sandwiches and surprising Drake at lunch. She nixed the idea as soon as she thought it and left the diner.

The last thing she wanted was to appear desperate. He'd slowed things down last night when she'd practically begged to speed it up.

Slow was good. She didn't want to get into another toxic relationship that sucked the life out of her.

Drake was nothing like her last boyfriend, Miles. Drake was so much more. He'd been a Navy SEAL. That took discipline, courage and strength. He valued the men he'd fought with and considered them brothers. He'd stepped in when Abby was in trouble and could kiss like nobody's business.

Cassie thought back to her first kiss with Miles. She couldn't even recall that kiss or any other they'd shared. They must have been as unremarkable as the man himself.

The more she compared Drake to Miles, the more she looked forward to seeing Drake again that night. With the condom her brother had given her, she'd be ready for whatever might happen. Only, this time, he'd have to initiate. He had to be just as ready and willing as she was.

She drove to the sheriff's office, parked and went inside.

"It's your day off," Sheriff Barron grumbled from inside his office. "You should be out riding horses, shopping with your gal pals, fishing or something. Not spending more time in this office."

"And when do you take time off?" she shot back at him.

He didn't answer.

"Right. Never." She slipped into one of the empty desks in the office across from the sheriff's. "Anything from the coroner?"

"Nothing," the sheriff said. "However, Molly

found old blueprints in the lodge office with notes made during previous remodeling efforts and building additions. The last remodel effort was fifteen years ago. The addition was twenty-one years ago when they added rooms to the west wing and expanded the kitchen."

Cassie powered up the computer and waited for it to come online. "That's a start. I'll dig into the missing persons database going back between fourteen and twenty-five years ago to bracket those timeframes."

Once she'd logged on, she brought up the Montana Missing Persons Database and went to work, sifting through hundreds of women with blond hair who'd gone missing during the ten-year span in which major modifications had been made within the lodge.

The number was too many. She narrowed the search to within a two-hundred-mile radius of Eagle Rock. That knocked the number down even more, but it was still too many to wade through one by one. A two-hundred-mile radius would lean into the neighboring state of Wyoming, which meant going into Wyoming's missing persons database. If she did it right, she'd also tap into the national database NamUs for women who might have been in transit through Montana on their way to Washington, Oregon, Idaho or Minnesota.

Overwhelmed by the sheer number of people

who'd gone missing during those years, Cassie focused on the Montana database. If she struck out there, she'd expand beyond the state. If only she had more to go on, like an age range, a birthmark or a tattoo. Dental records would be helpful when they narrowed it down to under twenty potential victims.

Though she was searching for the proverbial needle in the haystack, she couldn't sit around and do nothing. She'd run out of leads on Penny's case, but maybe, she could make headway on Jane Doe's. She'd joined the sheriff's department hoping to make a difference. In this case, they had a body. Surely, they'd be able to identify her and give her a proper burial and her family the closure they needed.

CASSIE READ through file after file, heartsick at the number of women who had never made it home from school, work or going for a freaking walk. Photo after photo of smiling blondes scrolled across her screen, ranging in age from ten to seventy-five, and she was no closer to naming the victim found in the Lucky Lady Lodge.

A sandwich arrived at noon, reminding Cassie she hadn't eaten breakfast. She'd only left her chair twice —once to use the bathroom, another time to warm up her cold coffee in the station's microwave. Sheriff Barron came in a couple of times to check on her but left to answer calls. The department was short-handed. He did what he could to fill the gaps. One call was a domestic disturbance at the local laundromat. Another time he left to help a woman herd her escape-artist donkey back into his pen.

There never a dull moment in Eagle Rock and the surrounding county. Cassie was grateful nothing major cropped up during the day. She'd have jumped in to help, on duty or not.

Nearing the end of the day, she was ready to admit defeat. She needed more information from the medical examiner before she could make any headway whatsoever.

The only bright spot to the day was that she would be seeing Drake again.

# CHAPTER 7

Drake spent the day much like the day before, tearing down walls damaged by the explosion. By mid-day, the men had completed the initial demolition needed to expose structural supports on the mountainside of the lodge. They stopped to take a break for lunch. Molly had packed food and drinks for the crew. They sat outside on the porch, breathing fresh air and discussing their progress.

"The structural engineer should be here after lunch to inspect the support beams," Molly said. "If he doesn't have time to complete his inspection today, he will return in the morning."

"Will we need to be out of the way while the structural engineer is conducting his inspection?" Drake asked.

"Only out of the rooms he'll be inspecting," Parker said. "As of now, we won't be tearing down any more walls unless the engineer thinks he needs to see more. We want the dust to settle enough he can see what he's doing, which means we'll move on to less dust-producing tasks until the engineer has completed his work."

Molly picked up the conversation. "Once we have his report, we can determine our next steps as far as walls and ceilings are concerned. In the meantime, we'll move to flooring. If we can salvage the original wood floors, we will. Where we can't, we'll need to rip out the damaged boards and prep for new flooring. The electrician will begin refitting damaged electrical lines tomorrow and bring anything that's substandard up to code." She smiled at the men. "Any of you ready to jump ship and join Hank's Brotherhood Protectors?"

"I, for one, want to see this project through to completion," Drake said.

The other men nodded their agreement.

Molly laughed. "Good. I'll need all of you to make our deadline of this fall. That's only a few months away. Barring any major setbacks, we should make that date."

They were collecting their discarded wrappers and drink bottles when two white trucks pulled up in the parking lot in front of the lodge.

One of the trucks bore a logo for Strong Engineering. A man with salt-and-pepper hair stepped down with a clipboard in his hand.

The second pickup sported the logo for Greenway Construction. The man who climbed down from that truck crossed to the first guy, shook hands and followed him up to the lodge.

Molly met the man with the clipboard at the top of the porch steps. "Doug, thank you for making time in your busy schedule." She shook hands with the man and turned to the men gathered around. "This is my demolition team. Guys, this is Douglas Strong of Strong Engineering. He might have questions for you as he goes." She turned to the man behind Doug and shook his hand. "Frank, I'm glad you could make it. We're still comparing bids and haven't awarded the contract, but we'd like to get your take on the work that will need to be done. Guys, this is Frank Matson, the owner of Greenway Construction."

Frank shook her hand, and then Parker's, and nodded to the men gathered around.

Molly and Parker led the men through the rooms where the special operations demolition team had cleared the debris away from the walls against the mountain.

Drake and the others worked on the floors in the kitchen, where they broke up cracked tile, loaded it into wheelbarrows and removed it from the building.

Thirty minutes into their work, Parker appeared in the kitchen.

"Drake."

Drake wiped the dust from his hands onto his

jeans and followed Parker through the dining room into the first room he'd worked. The one with the hidden room where he'd found the body.

Doug Strong held out his hand. "I understand you're a Navy SEAL."

Drake nodded and shook the man's hand.

"I did six years in the Navy. A recruiter convinced me to join the Navy and see the world." He laughed. "I spent all six years in the belly of a nuclear submarine and then used my GI bill to get my engineering degree. Now, I can't get enough fresh air and sunshine."

"I don't know how you did it. I wouldn't want to spend one year, much less six in a tin can."

"And I wouldn't want to walk into a hive of Taliban." He grinned. "Yet here we are in the Crazy Mountains of Montana." His smile faded. "Tell me about this wall."

Drake explained how he'd torn away the plaster from the other sections, but when he got to a gap, he had broken through what had appeared to be a doorway into a stone-walled room carved out of the mountainside.

"The good news is that the stone is intact. No cracks or damage of any kind. The solid rock probably shielded this room from the explosion in the mine, sparing the beam any structural damage. This room and the ones above it should be good to go." Doug shot a glance toward Molly.

"Are you going to keep the stone room open or seal it?"

Molly's gaze met Drake's. "I haven't decided. It's part of the lodge's history. I'd love to know what it was used for, but a body being discovered in it might be too creepy for our clientele. We hope to attract families." She shrugged. "I guess, to be determined."

Molly turned to Frank Matson. "Greenway Construction was one of the contractors who did some work during the addition twenty years ago and the remodel fifteen years ago. Did you keep records of the employees who worked the jobs?"

Frank shook his head. "You'll have to talk to Margaret Keller, my office manager. I didn't own the company back then. It belonged to my father-in-law. I bought him out when he retired twelve years ago. I doubt the employee records go back that far. I only keep mine for ten years and then purge. I'm almost sure those records were part of my ten-year purge." He frowned. "Do you think one of my father-in-law's guys sealed the woman in the stone room?"

Molly's gaze met Drake's. "Someone put her there and then covered the door with plaster. It had to have happened during one of the construction phases. The lodge was continuously operational otherwise. Someone would've noticed work being done in one of the rooms. It was just a thought."

And an avenue they'd have to explore. If one of the construction crew had sealed the woman inside the wall, she must've been dead at the time. Otherwise, she could've knocked through the plaster wall with little effort. If she'd been dead, and all signs indicated that was the case, most likely, she'd been murdered. Why else hide her body behind a wall?

Which meant someone had gotten away with murder and could still be living among the good citizens of Eagle Rock.

Drake glanced at his watch. "I need to talk with Frank's office manager and find out if the employment records had been purged when Frank bought the business from his father-in-law."

Parker led the engineer and Matson into the next room. Molly hung back, her gaze meeting Drake's. "You're taking this personally, aren't you?"

He nodded. "Yes, ma'am. I guess I am."

"I can't blame you. I suppose I would as well if I'd been the one to find the body." Molly kicked at a chunk of plaster. "You think Frank's office manager can help?"

Drake nodded. "Yes, ma'am."

"It's almost quitting time. You'd better hurry before his office closes. I'll let the others know you left for the day."

"Thank you." He left the lodge, climbed into his truck and raced into Eagle Rock, disregarding the speed limits. His first stop was the sheriff's office. Hopefully, he'd find Cassie there. She'd planned on spending the day searching the missing persons databases.

As he parked, he glanced at his watch again. Fifteen minutes until five o'clock. That didn't give him much time. But he knew Cassie would want to be there to question the office manager. She had more right to investigate than he did.

When Drake entered the sheriff's office, the front desk was empty. "Hello?" he called out.

"Drake?" Cassie's voice sounded first, and then she appeared in the doorway of an office. "What are you doing here? I thought you didn't get off until five o'clock?"

"I left early. Are you at a stopping point?"

She nodded. "I was just shutting down for the day."

"Do you know where Greenway Construction's office is?"

She nodded. "It's at the south end of town, several blocks from here. Why?"

"Greenway did the work on the addition twenty years ago, as well as the remodel five years later. Molly and I thought it would be a good idea to see if they kept employee records going that far back. But if we don't hurry, their shop will be closed before we get there, and we'll have to wait until morning to ask."

Cassie pulled the office door shut. "I'm ready.

Let's go." She followed him out of the sheriff's office and locked the door behind them.

Drake had left his truck running. Cassie ran for the passenger door while Drake hopped into the driver's seat. He spun out of the parking lot onto Main Street, heading south.

They were just pulling into the parking lot when a young woman with dark brown hair, wearing jeans and a polo shirt with the Greenway logo on the breast pocket, came out of the office, turned and locked the door.

Cassie was out of her seat before Drake engaged the parking brake. "Tacey, are you closing up shop for the night?"

Tacey smiled a greeting. "Sure am. Gotta get my son to his baseball practice. Is there something you need?"

"Hopefully, you can help us," Cassie turned to Drake. "By the way, this is Drake, my…boyfriend."

Drake fought the smile threatening to spread across his face at Cassie's quickly blurted lie.

Her cheeks flushed a pretty pink, making her freckles stand out. "Do you know if Greenway Construction kept employee records from a couple of jobs they did for the Lucky Lady Lodge fifteen and twenty years ago?"

Tacey shook her head. "I know where every sheet of paper is in that office. I reorganized everything when Frank hired me to replace Margaret Finley when she retired. I purged everything over ten years old, except for blueprints and building permits. If the employee records from fifteen and twenty years ago were in there, they were purged. I don't know how Margaret kept that office running as efficiently as she did. I couldn't find anything. She had her own way of filing things. Most of which was in her head."

Tacey's face brightened. "If you want to know anything about the projects Greenway constructed, where they were and who worked them, I'd ask Margaret." Tacey jingled her keys. "Now, I have a little boy waiting for his mama to take him to practice." She stepped past Cassie and Drake, climbed into her car and drove away.

"Where can we find Margaret Finley?" Drake asked as he climbed into his truck and started the engine.

Cassie settled into the seat beside him and buckled her seatbelt. "Margaret lives in a little house on the last street before you head out of Eagle Rock. Not far from here and next to the graveyard."

Drake's brow wrinkled. "That's a bit creepy."

Cassie hiked her eyebrows up and gave him a look. "Creepier than finding a body in a hidden room in the lodge?"

"Maybe not." He drove to the last street at the end of Eagle Rock and stopped in front of the house next to the graveyard.

A woman with white hair sat on the porch snapping green beans. Her eyebrows rose up her forehead. "Cassie Douglas, have you come to arrest me for the illegal cannabis I'm growing in a flowerpot on my back porch?"

"Margaret," Cassie said, shaking her head, "I didn't hear that."

The older woman chuckled. "Just kidding. I have a brown thumb. That cannabis plant died last summer because I didn't water it enough. I can't grow anything. I had to buy these green beans at the farmer's market." She smiled at Drake. "Did you bring me a present?"

Cassie laughed. "Margaret, you're incorrigible."

"That one of those words you picked up in law school?" She snorted. "When are you going back to finish your degree and get your license to practice?"

"I haven't yet decided."

"I'm waiting to commit some petty crime so you can represent me in court. Gotta support my peeps, don't I?" She patted the chair beside her. "Come sit. Haven't had a good chat with you since margarita night at the Blue Moose."

Cassie climbed the porch steps and dropped into the chair. "Margaret, this is Drake Morgan, former Navy SEAL, currently working with Molly McKinnon at the Lucky Lady Lodge."

"Oh." Margaret's eyes widened. "Are you the one who found the body?"

"That would be me." Drake joined the women on

the porch and held out his hand to Margaret. "Nice to meet you."

She rubbed her hand on the side of her jeans before taking his hand in a firm grip. "The pleasure is all mine. I can assure you."

"We stopped by the Greenway office just a minute ago and spoke with Tacey. She sent us to you."

Margaret snorted. "Can't she find anything since she reorganized the office?"

Cassie smiled. "We're trying to identify employees of Greenway who worked on projects at the Lucky Lady Lodge fifteen and twenty years ago."

"You think one of our employees might have left that body in the wall?" Margaret's eyes grew wider, and then she nodded thoughtfully. "It would make sense. They hadn't done any other upgrades or updates to the building since then." She snapped a bean into the bowl in front of her. "What do you want to know?"

"Who were your guys skilled with drywall installation?" Drake asked. "It takes skill to do it right."

Margaret nodded and then shook her head. "Yes and no. It doesn't take any skill to hang it, but it takes skill to float it and make it seamless." She grinned. "Earl Hensley. He was Greenway's best drywall guy."

"Was?" Drake questioned.

Cassie responded. "He's now Eagle Rock's best mechanic. I didn't know he hung drywall."

Margaret snapped another bean into the bowl.

"He and Frank had a falling out about the time Earl's older brother had a heart attack, died and left his auto repair shop to Earl." Margaret frowned. "I can't picture Earl killing anyone and hiding the body behind a wall. He's one of the nicest men I know. I'd have had him if he'd shown the least bit of interest."

Drake chuckled, and Cassie blushed.

"He never married." Margaret tilted her head to the side. "I always imagined some woman broke his heart. Maybe she did, and he stuffed her in the wall." The old woman shrugged. "You'll have to ask him. He might be working late. He usually does."

Drake met Cassie's gaze.

Margaret smiled. "I guess you'll be going. Thanks for stopping by and keeping me company for a few short minutes. Next time, stay a while and bring margaritas."

"You're on." Cassie bent to hug the woman. "Stay ornery. It suits you."

"Damn right, it does. Arthur Greenway understood me. We worked well together for over thirty years. Never had the same connection with Frank. Fortunately, I saved my pennies, invested in the stock market and retired with enough money to keep me in margaritas for a long time." She reached for Cassie's hand. "I hope you find out who she was and give her family some peace. And then nail the bastard who did that to her."

Cassie nodded solemnly. "That's the plan."

"And while you're at it, bring pretty Penny home where she belongs," Margaret said.

Cassie responded with a nod, her eyes glassy, swimming with tears.

Drake slipped an arm around her and led her back to the truck. He opened the door for her and helped her into the passenger seat.

His heart squeezed hard in his chest at the sadness in her eyes. Her friend Penny meant a lot to her. He wished he could help her in the search to find her.

"Which way?" he asked as he slipped behind the steering wheel and backed out of the driveway onto the road.

Cassie swallowed hard before she answered. After she gave him directions to Earl's auto repair shop, she sat back in her seat and stared out the front windshield.

"I stopped asking *why* a few weeks in as a sheriff's deputy," Cassie said softly. "Why are people so mean to each other? Why would someone kill another person? Why would someone want to harm an innocent child? Why would a person torture a dog?"

A single tear slipped down her cheek.

She wiped the tear away, her jaw hardening. "Asking why doesn't fix broken people. It doesn't make them nicer. Sometimes, I think I'm becoming too jaded and starting to think there is no goodness in this world." A smile tugged at the corner of her lips. "Then a handsome SEAL comes to the rescue of a stranger, making sure she's not harmed by one of those crazy people I don't understand. And an old woman invites me to her house for company and margaritas." She shot a watery smile toward Drake. "And my faith in humankind is renewed until the next dumbass does something heinous."

Drake reached across the console and took her hand in his. "I've had moments like that, more often than I care to admit. I can't dwell on those. Not when the sun keeps coming up in the morning, giving me a brand-new shot at a better day."

Cassie squeezed his hand. "You're all right, Drake Morgan. Look at us philosophizing, and we haven't even had any alcohol."

Drake laughed as he turned onto the street where Earl's auto repair shop stood, surrounded by several vehicles in various stages of assembly or disassembly.

Three large overhead doors graced the shop. Two were closed; one was wide open.

Drake parked in front of the shop and pushed his door open. As he stepped down, a scream echoed inside the open bay door, and a plump, gray-haired woman burst from the shadowy interior.

# CHAPTER 8

CASSIE DROPPED down from the truck and ran toward the screaming woman. She collapsed against her, sobbing wildly.

"Take a deep breath," Cassie said.

The woman sucked in a shaky breath then burst into tears again, pointing toward the shop.

"I'll check it out," Drake said.

"Do you have a gun?" Cassie asked softly, mouthing the words more than saying them out loud.

He nodded, reached into his truck, pulled a Glock out of the glove box and hurried toward the open bay door. He approached from the side, easing into the shadows.

Cassie's heart lodged in her throat when he disappeared into the building. She didn't breathe until he reappeared less than a minute later, his face grim, his lips pressed together in a tight line.

He walked toward her and the sobbing woman, then passed them, continuing to the truck. He pulled his cell phone out of the console and placed a call. "This is Drake Morgan. I'm at Earl Hensley's auto repair shop. Earl Hensley is dead, crushed beneath an auto lift."

Cassie gasped, and the woman in her arms sobbed louder.

Drake ended the call and joined Cassie.

"Let me," he said.

Cassie untangled the woman's arms from around her neck and turned her toward Drake. He handed her his gun and pulled the woman into his arms.

Cassie went into the auto repair shop, dreading what she'd find yet having to see for herself.

Just as Drake had reported to Marnie, the 911 dispatcher, Earl Hensley was dead, crushed beneath an auto lift with a full-sized SUV balanced on the rails. His eyes were wide open, as was his mouth as if he'd screamed in pain.

Cassie's stomach roiled. She turned and hurried out of the shop.

The wail of sirens sounded from the fire station as a fire truck and ambulance made their way toward them.

Within the next five minutes, the road filled with a fire truck, ambulance, the sheriff's vehicle and an array of personal vehicles driven by various volunteer firefighters and paramedics.

Sheriff Barron insisted on leaving the body until the state crime lab could get someone out there to process the scene. Though having a lift fall on Earl could have been an accident, he insisted on processing it as a homicide.

"Rather have a little overkill than miss evidence that could convict a killer," the sheriff said.

The sobbing woman was someone visiting relatives in Eagle Rock. Hers was the SUV on the rack. It was supposed to have been ready for pickup at five o'clock. When she'd arrived, she found Earl just as Drake and Cassie had. Crushed. Dead.

Representatives from the state crime lab arrived an hour and a half later.

The sheriff told Cassie that she and Drake could leave. She had to work the next day, and they didn't have anyone to fill in if she couldn't.

Tired and disheartened, she left with Drake, riding in silence until he pulled into the parking lot at the Blue Moose Tavern.

"I don't think I could eat a thing," she said. "But I'll sit with you while you grab a bite." The image of Earl squished beneath the lift could not be unseen.

Drake shifted into park and turned toward her, taking her hand in his. "I thought we'd get something light to eat and something strong to drink."

"I could go for that," she said.

He released her hand and climbed out of the truck. She didn't wait for him to come around to open her door. It was silly to sit there when they could both get inside sooner. She joined him at the front of the truck and slipped her hand inside his. By now, she didn't give a damn who saw her. She wanted the comfort holding his hand brought. It wasn't like it made them a thing.

Abby saw them as they entered and hurried over to the hostess. "I'll seat them in my area."

The hostess nodded and handed her the menus.

Abby showed them to a booth half hidden near the back of the restaurant. She set the menus on the table in front of them and grimaced. "I heard about what happened. Can I get you both a whiskey neat?"

"Make it a double," Cassie said.

"Same," Drake added.

Abby nodded and hurried away to get their drinks.

Cassie sat staring at the menu without seeing it. Earl's eyes were forever etched in her mind.

"Do you think someone killed him?" Cassie whispered.

Drake nodded. "Those lifts are safety rated. They don't fall."

"Someone had to have lowered it onto Earl," Cassie said. "But who?"

He didn't want to say it but felt he had to. "He had to incapacitate Earl first. The lift would've gone down slowly."

Abby arrived with the whiskey and set it on the

table in front of them. "What can I get you two to eat?" she asked.

Drake ordered a chicken salad with an extra plate and fork. "We'll start there. If we're still hungry, we can order something else."

Abby nodded and hurried away to fill the order.

Cassie shook her head. "I don't think I'll ever be hungry again."

Drake reached across the table and took her hands in his. "The memory will fade."

He would know, she thought. He had to have seen much worse in battle.

She had to pull it together. A sheriff's deputy couldn't fall apart over a crushed mechanic. Cassie sat up straighter and squared her shoulders. "I have to work the day shift tomorrow. By the time we eat, it will be too late to go stargazing."

Drake nodded. "I figured as much. It'll also be late for you to drive home and then back at O-dark-thirty in the morning. You should stay in town tonight."

"I have no desire to camp out in the sheriff's station, even if there is a cot stashed in the far corner of the storage room. I need a real bed with a real pillow."

"I have one of each." Drake grinned. "A bed and a pillow. I even have a small couch." He squeezed her hands. "Stay with me. I promise to let you sleep."

Sharing a bed with him would not equal sleep.

She frowned, but the invitation was out there now, and she couldn't just brush it aside. Not when she wanted to take him up on it and spend the night lying naked in his arms. Heat coiled low in her belly and radiated throughout her body.

Staying with him would also help her banish the image of Earl. If she went home to the ranch, she'd lie awake well into the night, afraid to close her eyes for fear that every time she did, she'd see Earl's sightless eyes staring back at her.

"Okay," she murmured softly.

"And if you stay, you won't have as far to drive in the morning. Which means you will get to sleep a little longer."

Her lips twitched. "I said okay."

Drake laughed. "You did, didn't you?"

She arched an eyebrow. "You didn't think I would."

"I wasn't sure after I pretty much rejected you last night." He lifted her hand to his lips. "You should know I had to take two ice-cold showers before I could even consider sleep."

"Good. So did I."

He held up a hand. "But we can just sleep. You and I both have to work tomorrow."

Cassie nodded. "Yeah, we'll sleep." She almost laughed at the absurdity of thinking they'd only sleep. She had a condom in her back pocket. She'd left the ranch that morning with every intention of putting that condom to use. Drake couldn't use the lack of protection as an excuse to abstain. If he really wanted her, she was ready. She lifted the glass of whiskey to her lips and sipped the amber liquid, letting the alcohol burn down her throat, warming her insides.

Abby appeared, carrying the salad, extra plates and utensils.

Cassie placed one of the empty plates in front of her and scooped lettuce and chicken onto it.

Drake did the same and poured dressing from a little plastic cup onto the leafy greens.

They ate in silence, Cassie nibbling like a rabbit on the lettuce and spinach leaves. She ate a couple of bites of chicken, determined to get some protein in her system to keep up her strength. If they put the condom to use, she wanted to give as good as she got. Still no hungrier, she forced down enough fuel to sustain her until lunch the following day.

When she'd had enough, she laid down her fork, picked up her glass of whiskey and sipped.

Drake lifted the last bite of the salad to his lips and chewed slowly.

Cassie wanted to scream. "You're teasing me, right?"

He grinned. "Is it working?"

"If by working you mean, I'm ready to leave, and you're taking too long, then yes."

He shook his head. "No. Is it working?"

That heat low in her belly flared into an inferno. If they didn't leave soon, she might have to drag him into the ladies' room, block the door and make love against the wall.

His bed with pillows would be much easier and less public.

"Okay," she said. "Yes. It's working." She shifted in her seat, hotter than she'd ever been and still fully dressed.

Abby appeared with the bill.

While she waited for Drake to pull his credit card from his wallet, the younger woman grinned broadly. "I got my DNA results back this afternoon. I can't wait to go over them and then log into the ancestry database.

"I logged on this morning just to learn how to navigate. My results hadn't been released yet. Hopefully, by morning, my data will be merged on my profile, and I'll be able to trace back through my ancestors."

"It's a cool undertaking," Cassie said. "A friend of mine who was adopted found her birth mother through one of the ancestry databases. Sadly, her birth mother had passed. Still, she was able to locate half-brothers and sisters, so she went from being an only child to being one of fourteen. She was so happy to have found family."

"Wouldn't it be neat to find aunts, uncles and cousins?" Abby clasped her hands together. "It will also be interesting to see which of my relatives has lupus, dementia and Alzheimer's. Maybe they'll have advice on how to deal with all of it." Abby took Drake's credit card. "I'll be right back."

"I hope Abby's relatives will be as happy to get to know her as she will be to know them," Cassie said, her gaze following the kind-hearted young woman who only wanted an extended family to love. With a father who worked long hours and a mother who didn't recognize her, she was likely starved for affection.

Cassie could relate.

Abby returned with Drake's card and receipt. He signed the slip, slipped his card into his wallet, pushed to his feet and held out his hand. "Ready?"

"I am." She placed her hand in his and left the tavern.

In silence, he held her door for her, his hands lightly touching her as he helped her up into her seat.

Then he jogged around to the other side and climbed up into his seat.

Cassie's pulse sped up as they left the tavern and drove the short distance to Ms. Dottie Kinner's B&B.

Once again, she allowed him to open the door for her, even though she was fully capable of doing it herself. As he helped her to the ground, she asked. "How does Ms. Dottie feel about you entertaining a woman in your room?"

Drake frowned. "I hadn't thought about it. I

consider it like a hotel room. What I do behind my closed door is my business—as long as I don't disturb others." He touched a hand to the small of her back and leaned close. "You're not a screamer, are you?"

Cassie laughed, her body super sensitive to his touch. She couldn't wait to get inside and behind his closed door. Unfortunately, they might have to run the gauntlet of the other guests if they weren't already in their rooms for the night.

Drake led her up the porch stairs and held the door for her as she stepped into the house.

The front room with the sofa and wing-backed chairs was empty. So far, so good.

Voices sounded from the other side of the dining room, coming from the kitchen she'd been in several times as a child when her mother had come to one of Ms. Dottie's teas.

The voices grew louder as if they were coming toward them.

Drake handed her the key. "Go while I run interference."

Cassie sprinted for the staircase and stopped with her foot on the first riser. "Which room?"

"Second door on the right. I'll be up as soon as possible." He turned away from her and hurried for the kitchen.

Cassie ran up the stairs and fumbled with fitting the key into the lock on the second door to the right.

Below her, Drake said, "Having a party without me?"

Another male voice responded, "Ms. Dottie broke out a bottle of Scotch whiskey. We couldn't let her drink alone."

"Murdock, I've never known you to turn down an offer of Scotch," Drake said.

"Pretty damn fine whiskey, too," another man commented. "Ms. Dottie has good taste in Scotch."

Ms. Dottie's laughter carried up to the second floor. "You don't get to be my age without finding the good stuff. Care for some?"

Drake chuckled. "I would, except I've already had my limit for a work night. I'm headed for a shower and bed."

Cassie twisted the key in the lock and tried to turn the handle. It didn't move.

The voices and footsteps moved closer.

Cassie counted the number of doors. She had turned right at the top of the stairs and gone to the second door on the right. She tried again. The door didn't budge.

Muttering a silent curse, she ran back to the top of the stairs and kept going as if she'd turned left instead of right and found the second door on the right. The key fit in easily, and the door opened.

She stepped through it and closed the door softly behind her, leaving it unlocked for when Drake finally came up.

A quick inspection of the room assured her it had everything they needed. There was even a stash of condoms inside the nightstand. A thrill of anticipation stormed through her. Making love once was all she could hope for, but the possibilities seemed endless with a drawer full of protection.

She considered slipping into the shower but wasn't sure how noisy the pipes were or how many other guests occupied the B&B besides Drake and his teammates. If she fired up the shower, and they were Ms. Dottie's only guests, they'd know for sure someone else was in the building beside them.

Cassie wasn't sure why she cared whether they knew of not. But the secrecy and sneaking around really amped up the excitement to the point she was ready to get the party started.

Footsteps sounded on the stairs.

Her breath stalled in her lungs, and Cassie listened carefully, trying to decide if they turned left or right.

Definitely left and headed her way.

She stood in the middle of the room, her heart racing. What if she'd entered the wrong room? What if Drake had changed his mind?

The doorknob turned, and the door swung open.

Drake stepped through, calling over his shoulder. "See you in the morning."

"Hey, Drake?"

"Yeah, Grimm," Drake turned to address his friend in the hallway.

"You might ask your lady friend if she wants a glass of that damned fine Scotch whiskey."

Laughter rang out in the hallway.

Drake shook his head. "Assholes."

"The kitchen window looks out onto the street. We saw you and your woman get out of your truck. Don't worry. Ms. Dottie's cool as long as you don't get the bedsprings squeaking."

More laughter sounded, and footsteps moved away.

Drake entered the room, closed the door and gave her a crooked grin. "You heard them. You could have had a glass of damned fine Scotch whiskey."

She closed the distance between them, reached around Drake and twisted the lock on the doorknob.

Then she stood in front of him. "I'm not interested in drinking scotch with your friends." She pulled his T-shirt from the waistband of his jeans.

Drake gripped her arms and stopped her there. "Sweetheart, I want to hold you so badly I hurt. But I need a shower before we go any further."

"Perfect. So do I." She pulled her blouse over her head and tossed it across the sofa by the window. Then she dragged his T-shirt over his head.

He tossed it aside and reached for the button on her jeans, flicking it through the hole. Then he eased the zipper down and slipped his hand inside to cup her sex.

Her breath hitched as bursts of electricity zipped through her, making her body tingle. Her breathing grew ragged, and her need more urgent.

When she tried to loosen the button on his jeans, she fumbled. Drake brushed her fingers aside, flicked the button free, dropped the zipper and stepped out of his jeans.

She reached behind her back and unhooked her bra, letting it slide off her shoulders and down her arms.

His eyes flared as he dragged her jeans over her hips and downward until they pooled around her ankles, and she stepped free, kicking them aside.

Then he scooped her into his arms and strode across the room into the bathroom.

Setting her on her feet, he reached into the shower, turned on the water and adjusted the temperature. When it was warm enough, he took her hand and stepped beneath the spray, bringing her with him.

Cassie poured shampoo into her hand, built the lather, and then rubbed it into his hair. The suds slithered over his shoulders and across his chest.

Her hands followed, sliding over every inch, exploring hard muscles encased in smooth skin. As the soap carried away the dust of his day's work, she pushed him beneath the spray, letting it rinse away the bubbles.

She poured body wash into her palm and worked it across his torso, moving downward to the hardened evidence of his desire.

Cassie circled her hands around his cock, reveling in how long, thick and hard it was. She wanted him. Inside her. Soon.

But first...her hands moved up and down his length in a slow, steady rhythm. When all the soap had washed away, Cassie dropped to her knees in front of him. The shower's spray peppered her face and head as she touched her tongue to the tip of his shaft and drew a line around the rim. She wrapped her lips around him and flicked the tiny hole, teasing and licking.

Drake dug his hands into her damp hair, his fingers pressing into her scalp.

Cassie gripped his buttocks and pulled him close, taking his cock into her mouth and swallowing as much as she could of him until he bumped against the back of her throat.

He held still for a long moment and then slid back out.

She flicked the tip of his cock with her tongue and then tightened her hold around his hips and pulled him back into her mouth. Then back out and back in until he took over and set the pace.

Cassie's fingers dug into his ass, holding on as he

pumped in and out, increasing the speed and intensity with every stroke.

His muscles tightened, and his breathing grew labored.

Cassie loved that she was driving him to the edge of his control.

Drake pulled free, lifted Cassie to her feet and turned her into the shower's spray. "Your turn."

"But you're not there."

"I want to make this last a little longer. Let me please you." He squirted shampoo into his hand and massaged it into her scalp. Then he followed the bubbles over her shoulders and across her collarbone to her breasts. With the body wash, he lathered each breast, massaging them gently and then rolling the nipples between his thumb and forefinger until they hardened into tight little buttons.

His hands slipped lower, trailing across her torso, angling toward the juncture of her thighs and the tuft of hair covering her sex.

He cupped her and slid a finger into her channel, swirling around and around until she placed her hand over his and pressed more fingers into her channel. "I. Want. You."

"Soon," he promised.

She shook her head. "No. Now."

He chuckled, bent and scooped her up by the backs of her thighs and wrapped her legs around his waist.

His cock pressed against her entrance, yet he hesitated. "Damn."

"What?" She squirmed, trying to sink lower, desperate for him to enter her, fill her and make love to her.

"The protection is in the other room."

She moaned and pressed her breasts against his chest. Then she reached around him and turned off the shower. "Towel."

He grabbed a towel from the rack, set her on her feet and dried every inch of her body, lingering on her breasts and her sex. When he was done, she took a dry towel and swept it over his body, drying everything from the top of his head to the tips of his toes. When she was done, she took his hand, led him into the bedroom and stood beside the bed.

She leaned up on her toes and touched her lips to his.

He responded by wrapping his arms around her and crushing her body to his.

Cassie laced her fingers behind his neck, snuggled even closer and pressed the length of her naked body against his. Curling her calf behind his leg, she rubbed her sex across his thigh.

He growled deep in his chest. "I won't last much longer if you keep doing that."

"No holding back, baby," she said.

"I want you to go first," he whispered against her ear, sending shivers across her skin.

He scooped her up and laid her across the bed.

For a moment, he stood back, his gaze sweeping the length of her. "You're beautiful," he said.

She blushed. "I've never seen myself that way."

"I'm seeing you. You're beautiful, and I'm going to make you lose yourself."

A smile spread across her face. "Is that a challenge or a promise?"

"Both." He crawled over her and started his campaign with an assault of kisses, beginning with her mouth and spreading south to the swells of her breasts.

After tasting, touching and teasing each nipple until Cassie was squirming against the mattress, Drake moved lower, pressing his lips to each rib on his trek southward to the fluff of hair covering her lady bits.

With his thumbs, he parted her folds and touched her clit with the tip of his tongue.

She gasped and reached for his hair, weaving her fingers through his thick curls. What he inspired sent her soaring.

When he tongued her again, her breath caught and held.

Settling into his task, he focused on that nerve-packed flesh, touching, flicking and swirling until Cassie flew over the edge.

Her body pulsed with the force of her release, sending wave after wave of sensations throughout her body. She rode the orgasm for as long as she could. At last, she sank back to earth, her body still humming with her release.

Cassie collapsed against the mattress. But she wasn't done. She still had a void to be filled, and only Drake could do that.

She grabbed his hair and tugged gently.

Drake crawled up her body and settled between her knees, his cock pressing to her entrance.

He grabbed a condom from the drawer in the nightstand, tore it open and rolled it over his shaft. Positioning himself at her entrance, he slowly pressed into her.

Cassie raised her knees, dug her heels into the comforter and pushed her bottom upward, forcing Drake deeper.

When he pulled nearly all the way out, she lowered herself to the mattress. Then he was back again, filling her, moving in and out, faster and faster.

Drake thrust again and again until his body tensed. He drove deep and held, his cock pulsing against the walls of her channel.

Cassie lay against the mattress, a smile spreading across her face. This was what making love was all about. It was as if it had been her first time.

As Drake gathered her close, maintaining their intimate connection, Cassie snuggled closer, praying her first real orgasm would not be her last.

# CHAPTER 9

CASSIE WAS UP and out of Drake's room before five the next morning. He would have liked to snuggle a little longer and maybe make love again, but she'd been insistent she had to get to the sheriff's office early enough to change into her uniform and be ready for shift change at seven o'clock.

Drake suspected she hadn't wanted to run into the other guys and chose to leave before they started moving about. She'd promised to see him again that night.

Drake got up earlier than he had to but moved at a more leisurely pace since he had plenty of time to dress, eat breakfast and get to the job site by eight.

Where Cassie had managed to avoid his team-mates, Drake had to face them and Ms. Dottie over breakfast. He considered skipping and would have, had he not run into Murdock leaving his room at the same time as Drake.

Murdock grinned. "Morning, lover boy."

"Shut up, Murdock," Drake grumbled.

"You know these walls are pretty thin. We could hear her screams all night long."

"Liar," Drake said. "She isn't a screamer."

"Ha!" Murdock's grin broadened. "So she did stay the night, and you did do the nasty."

Drake glared at the man. "Shut the fuck up before I put a pre-coffee fist in your face."

Murdock shielded his face. "Not the face, dude. I hope to make beautiful children someday, and I'll need this face to attract a beautiful baby mama." He dropped his hands and headed for the stairs. "Are you working at the lodge today or following up on the investigation with the deputy?"

"Going to the lodge, as far as I know."

"Molly and Parker are anxious to resolve the issue of the Jane Doe murder. They fear the murder will discourage clients from staying at the Lucky Lady Lodge."

"Are you kidding? News of the murder will bring every nut case amateur detective who'll want in on the action."

"They're afraid others won't come because the lodge could be haunted by the murder victim."

Drake chuckled. "Which will bring every ghost hunter across the country to Eagle Rock and the

Lucky Lady Lodge to see the ghost of the very unlucky lady."

Murdock laughed as he followed Drake down the stairs. "I thought it was Grimm's job to be morbidly funny. When did you gain the art of sarcasm?"

"After I left the Navy and went to work as a mercenary in Afghanistan. You have to keep on your toes when you work with killers."

"Did I hear you say, killer?" Grimm asked from where he stood near the coffeemaker. "Have you gotten any more information on the body, her killer or the guy who off'd Eagle Rock's number one mechanic?"

"None of the above." Drake snagged a mug and filled it with hot, life-giving coffee.

Ms. Dottie emerged from the kitchen carrying a loaded tray filled with eggs, bacon, sausage, toast and a large bowl of oatmeal.

Grimm and Murdock hurried over to relieve the woman of her burden.

After setting the platters and bowls of food in the middle of the table, Ms. Dottie straightened. "I skipped the Danishes and opted for scrambled eggs for this morning's breakfast. Eggs and oatmeal are supposed to increase stamina and libido."

The gulp of coffee Drake had just taken spewed through his nose, setting off a coughing fit that lasted until his eyes watered and his lungs hurt.

Murdock pounded Drake on the back. "That's

right. Ms. D. knows all the foods you should eat before and after sex. It was quite the discussion in the kitchen last night over whiskey."

Grimm nodded. "She's practically an expert, having studied all the scientific journals about how to improve your sex life."

Ms. Dottie waved toward the table. "Eat before it gets cold. And just because I'm old doesn't mean I've given up on sex. I might have the body of a seventy-seven-year-old, but there's a forty-year-old vixen inside who thinks she's still in the prime of her life." She pulled out a chair and pointed at Drake. "Sit. You need to fuel your body. Sex can be exhausting."

Drake dropped into the seat. "Thank you, Ms. Dottie."

"You're welcome, my dear." She returned to the kitchen, leaving Grimm and Murdock snickering.

Drake shook his head. "I don't think I've ever had a morning in mixed company—and by mixed, I mean multi-generational—where the word sex was brought up not once but repeatedly before I'd consumed a full cup of coffee."

"I believe Ms. Dottie is my spirit grandmother." Murdock sat across from Drake and spooned eggs onto his plate and oatmeal into a smaller bowl. "I want to be like her when I'm that age."

Ms. Dottie came back in carrying a bowl of freshly sliced fruit. "Also good for the libido." She set it on the table and claimed the seat on the end.

Murdock sprang to his feet to help her with the chair.

Once everyone had food on their plates, Ms. Dottie glanced at Drake. "I'm beginning to think you attract bad juju, Mr. Morgan."

Drake looked up from the forkful of eggs suspended halfway to his mouth. "I'm sorry…what did you say?"

"Juju." She pointed her fork at him. "Since you've come to town, you've discovered a dead woman and our only decent mechanic crushed by the tools of his trade." She waved the fork. "I hate to ask what's next for you."

"It's not like I set out to find bodies," he said.

Her face softened. "I'm just yanking your chain. I'm a good judge of character. I know you wouldn't have committed those crimes. But someone did. It worries me to no end knowing there's a killer out there who has no regard for life."

"We're working on it," Drake said.

"Your sweetie is one smart cookie," Ms. Dottie said between bites. "Between you two, you'll find who is responsible for the two murders."

Drake hoped they would before any more lives were lost. He strongly suspected Earl's death was connected with the woman they'd found in the lodge. If he'd been targeted for something he might have known, how many other workers who'd been there for the addition and remodel would be at risk.

He needed to get back to Margaret Finley's place and pick her brain for more names. First, he had to show up for work. He'd promised to be there for the duration of the project. Today was only his third day on the job, and he was about to ask for time off so that he could chase more leads in the woman's death, and now Earl's, decades later.

He quickly ate the food provided, thankful for the nutrients that would help him get through the day and possibly the night. "Please excuse me. I have a lot of work to get through today."

"We're doing the same work," Grimm pointed out.

"Unless he's going to ask for the day off to help with the investigation," Murdock said. "I'm right, aren't I?"

"We'd go with you, but that would make Molly and Parker fall behind on their reno schedule," Grimm said.

Drake pushed back from the table and started to collect his plate and glass.

"Leave it," Ms. Dottie said. "Your time is better spent helping Deputy Douglas find killers."

He nodded to his host. "Thank you." To his teammates, he said, "We'll catch up later."

"Hey, Drake," Murdock raised a hand. "Don't forget Hank Patterson."

Drake frowned. "What about Hank?"

"He can help. He's got a computer guru who could help with the missing persons database. And if you need backup, you have his Brotherhood Protectors and us."

He'd forgotten about Hank and his protective service. He'd call him right after he talked with Molly.

He hurried up to his room, slipped his shoulder holster over his head and buckled it around his waist. His pistol was out in the truck. He'd holster it and take the gun wherever he went until they solved the crime and brought the killer to justice.

He brushed his teeth then ran down the stairs. Out in the parking lot, he climbed into his truck, shifted into drive and headed for the sheriff's office. He entered, hoping to find Cassie.

Sheriff Barron was there with a woman manning the telephone. Already the calls were coming in. The woman handled the calls quickly, professionally and with the skill and patience needed to walk the callers through what they could do to help their situations.

The sheriff held out his hand. "Deputy Douglas is out on a call investigating a drive-by mailbox bashing."

Drake shook the sheriff's hand. "If she returns anytime soon, tell her I'm headed to Margaret Finley's. I'm going to pick her brains for more names of employees who were there throughout the remodel and addition."

"I should come with you," the sheriff said.

"I can get the list and bring it back for you. You're

understaffed, and Molly made me available to help out."

"At the very least," Sheriff Barron reached into a drawer and pulled out a brass star with EAGLE ROCK SHERIFF'S DEPUTY engraved in the metal. "Let me deputize you. It might be important if we end up in court."

Drake shrugged. "Sure. Any words of wisdom?"

"Don't do anything illegal to collect any kind of evidence, or it won't be admissible in court."

"I'll keep that in mind."

Sheriff Barron came to attention.

Drake shot to attention, his body ramrod straight, chin up, shoulders back and his hands cupped at his sides.

"Raise your right hand," the sheriff said.

Drake raised his right hand, staring ahead, unmoving, serious.

"Do you so solemnly swear to uphold the values, laws and guidelines of the Eagle Rock Sheriff's Department, the laws of the State of Montana and the government of the United States of America?"

"I do," Drake said.

"I hereby appoint you as a Deputy." He pinned the star to Drake's chest, stood back and saluted.

Drake popped his best salute, pride swelling in his chest over that bronze star that could have easily come out of a kid's toy box.

Sheriff Barron clapped his hands together. "Now,

get out there and come up with some names of folks we can call on."

Drake left the office with the deputy's badge hanging crookedly on his T-shirt. Minutes later, he pulled onto the street where Margaret lived, slowing as he took in what appeared to be a disaster.

The cute white bungalow with the wide front porch looked nothing like it had the night before.

Someone had painted graffiti on almost every inch of the building's exterior, the windows, steps and decking.

Margaret stood on her porch with a hose and scrub brush, rubbing at the graffiti. "Damn kids have no respect for private property."

Drake climbed the steps and stood next to the older woman. "When did this happen?" He reached for her hand and held it as he inspected the splashes of red paint forming jagged words. His eyes narrowed. "Does that say what I think it says?"

Margaret nodded, her mouth forming a tight line. "Shut up or die." Her face was pale, and every hard-earned line seemed to have deepened since he'd seen her snapping beans on a clean porch the day before.

"I hadn't talked to anybody but you and Cassie since yesterday morning," she said, staring at the damage, the hose hanging at her side. "Now, sweet Earl is dead, and this happened overnight. I sleep with a noise machine to drown out the sounds of the cicadas. I didn't know I'd been tagged until I walked outside and found this."

"Do you need help scrubbing it off?" he asked.

She shook her head. "No. You need to get out there and find who's behind these attacks." She pulled a crumpled paper from her pocket and handed it to Drake. "After you two left last night, I figured you might be back for more names."

"That's why I'm here this morning," Drake concurred.

Margaret nodded toward the paper in his hands. "I think those are all the people who worked for Greenway on the two projects back then. We had other projects those years in Bozeman, Helena, Idaho Falls and Coeur d'Alene, Idaho. My memory is a little fuzzy, but that should give you a start for those who worked at the Lucky Lady Lodge. Some of those people still live in Eagle Rock. Others have moved. I noted the last places I knew where they might be found." She gave him a crooked, tired smile. "I hope it helps to nail the bastard."

Drake nodded. "Thank you for this," he said. "I'll get to work interviewing each of them."

Margaret touched a finger to the shiny bronze star. "I see you took a step on the wild side."

"The sheriff thought I might need a little clout to conduct interviews," Drake explained.

"A valid concern." Margaret smiled. "Thank you for taking the lead on this."

Drake grinned. "I can't take credit. It's been a team of people feeding information to Deputy Douglas. We're still waiting for the medical examiner's findings."

"I hope someone on that list can shed light on how that woman got where she was when you found her." She glanced at the paint on her walls. "It's not coming off. Looks like I'll be painting." She shrugged. "I was tired of white, anyway. I'm thinking eggplant purple with summer squash trim." She laughed. "That should have the historical society in fits."

Drake left Margaret talking to herself about paint colors and laughing out loud. He worried that she wasn't taking the threat seriously. After Earl's gruesome death, he wouldn't put it past the killer to make good on his threat and off the spunky septuagenarian.

First stop was, as promised, the sheriff's office, where he made a copy of the names, leaving one with the sheriff. They put their heads together to come up with addresses for those who still lived in the area.

"I'll give the rest of the list to Hank Patterson," Drake said. "From what I'm told, he has a computer guy who works miracles with databases."

Sheriff Barron snorted. "I suspect he engages in some forms of hacking to work those miracles. I can't prove it. Frankly, I don't want to. As long as his intentions are pure, I see no need to interfere. Besides, if one of my loved ones was in trouble, I'd pull every string, access every source, legal or not, to save them."

"Has Cassie asked Hank to help her find her friend Penny?" Drake asked.

The sheriff's brow puckered. "To my knowledge, she's never tapped on the Brotherhood Protectors as a resource in her search."

Drake's eyebrow rose. "Perhaps it's time...?"

"Perhaps." The sheriff took all the names of the men living on the south side of town." I'll check with each of them and slide by Margaret's place to see how she's doing."

"Good," Drake said. "I'm worried she's not doing enough to protect herself."

"She's a stubborn woman. I know for a fact she has a 357 magnum her first husband left her. He died of a heart attack when he was only thirty-seven years old, leaving her a widow at thirty-two." The sheriff shook his head. "Quite the looker, too. She had all the wives worried their husbands would stray."

"Did they?" Drake asked.

"Not with Margaret. She sought companionship in other towns and didn't bring them home to Eagle Rock. I think she never found someone she loved as much as her first husband."

"I like her," Drake said. "I'd hate to see her hurt."

"I'll do my best to check on her throughout the day."

Drake nodded. "But you're short-staffed. I'll go

through as many of these workers as I can. Just let me know which ones you get to so we don't overlap."

"Deal."

Drake walked with Sheriff Barron out of the office and stood on the sidewalk in front. "Where did you say Deputy Douglas was?"

"She's out at the Crooked Creek Ranch, checking on a potential property theft." Sheriff Barron grinned. "Bobby Joe Tarpin claims his still was stolen. I suspect his wife got tired of him spending more time with the still and his buddies than he was on chores and her. The deputy should be heading back before her shift ends at five."

That gave Drake several hours to work his way down the list.

He headed north while the sheriff turned south.

They might be chasing shadows, but doing something was better than doing nothing. And apparently, their poking around was stirring up trouble. Already, it had cost one life. Drake would emphasize to the men he interviewed that their lives could be in just as much danger as Earl's had been. That might get tongues wagging. Any clues, no matter how big or small, had to help.

Knowing the identity of the original victim was still the biggest clue of all that would help them find the one responsible.

He hoped that would happen soon, preferably before anyone else turned up dead.

# CHAPTER 10

THREE DAYS PASSED in which Cassie worked her shift patrolling the county, answering 911 calls and breaking up fights between family members. As soon as she got off duty, she went back to the office for a couple more hours to pour through the missing persons databases with no further breakthroughs regarding the woman in the wall.

To make it even more depressing, no more clues surfaced to help Cassie in her search to find her missing friend.

She'd always thought that a body was the most important and telling clue. They had the mummified remains of a woman. A body. And no idea who she was, nor how or why she'd been sealed in the hidden room behind the drywall.

Fishing through missing persons databases

seemed futile. With no distinctive features that would help her narrow her search to a more reasonable outcome, she was stuck looking through hundreds of entries with photos of women who'd disappeared fifteen to twenty years ago.

With Molly's permission to miss his day job, Drake had worked with the sheriff over the past couple of days, following through on the list of employees of Greenway Construction who'd been on the job during the work on the addition or the remodeling.

None of them admitted to hanging drywall sheets in that particular room on their own. That had been Earl's job. They'd helped him when it had come to lifting the heavy sheets of gypsum up to the high ceilings, but, for the most part, Earl had been there, directing the men in the proper way to fit full sheets of drywall against existing studs.

The sheriff and Drake hadn't been any more successful in their interviews than Cassie had been doing research in the databases.

Hank Patterson had offered his computer guru, Swede, to help sift through the missing persons databases. Cassie decided it was pointless to add more people when they didn't have the information about the body.

After Drake and the sheriff had exhausted the list of workers, Drake joined Cassie at the sheriff's office in the evenings, bringing her dinner from the B&B, provided by the talented Ms. Dottie, or a meal he'd ordered as carry-out from the Blue Moose Tavern.

They'd searched the databases, bouncing ideas and scenarios off each other, hoping one made sense.

After a few hours of fruitless data mining, they'd call it quits, drive over to the bed and breakfast, shower together and fall into bed.

Inevitably, they'd have a sudden burst of energy, fueled by desire. They made love and then fell asleep in each other's arms.

Being naked with Drake was the best part of Cassie's week. He was a thoughtful lover, always ensuring she climaxed first and then again when he was inside her.

Cassie considered less than a week was too soon to know where their relationship was headed. One thing was certain...they were good together. Working through issues, brainstorming ideas and making love. The kissing couldn't be better.

By Friday, Cassie was ready to drive to Missoula and shake information out of the medical examiner and the forensics team.

She'd taken her lunch break in the office, going through more images of smiling women who had never made it home. It was depressing and seemingly endless. After an afternoon of patrolling and performing her normal deputies' duties, she ended her shift and settled into the office.

An hour later, the front door of the sheriff's office squeaked open. Sheriff Barron was having dinner with the mayor and city council members to discuss the sad lack of applicants for the open positions in the sheriff's department.

Cassie called out, "Can I help you" and poked her head out of the office door.

Abby stood there with a paper in her hand, her brow puckered, appearing confused. When she saw Cassie, she sighed. "Oh, good. You're just the person I wanted to talk to. Is anyone else here?"

"It's just me minding the store," Cassie said. "Come on back."

Abby joined her in the office. Pulling up one of the rolling office chairs, she sat and placed the sheet of paper on the table in front of Cassie. "I don't get it."

Cassie stared down at three sets of data. "What is this?"

"You remember I told you I had my DNA analyzed?"

Cassie nodded.

"Are these your results?" She leaned over the sheet, curious about how it worked, having considered doing it herself.

"Mine, my father's…and my mother's."

Cassie glanced up. "How did you get your mother and father to participate? I thought your father was against it."

Abby's cheeks flushed a deep pink. "I told them I was doing an experiment for my biology class on the amount of bacteria in a person's spit. I wanted to see who I was most like." She sighed. "I know that wasn't very honest, but that's not what's got me concerned."

Cassie frowned down at the diagram. "Then what does?"

"I don't think it worked. Maybe I didn't give a good enough sample to work with, or I didn't get a good enough one from my mother."

"Why do you say that?" Cassie focused on the diagrams.

"I asked them to compare my DNA and that of my mother and father. I show a direct match with my father." She pointed to her father's graph, then moved her finger to the one labeled Linda Greenway Matson. "There's so little similarity between my mother's sample and mine that the test came back as no relation."

"Like you said, the sample might not have been good enough for them to run the comparison," Cassie said.

"But if they were able to identify the percentages of different origins, shouldn't they have been able to run a valid comparison?"

"These tests aren't foolproof."

Abby pushed to her feet. "They use DNA to convict rapists. I'd hope they're at least 99.9 percent correct." Her voice rose with her words. "What does it mean? If we aren't a match at all, I'm not her daughter. She's not my mother."

"Adoption?" Cassie suggested.

"I've seen copies of my birth certificate. It clearly states that Linda Matson was my mother." She paced the short distance across the little office, turned and paced back. "Why would they lie to me?"

Cassie hated seeing the happy, optimistic Abby so disturbed, but she couldn't fix this. "That's a question for your father."

Abby came to a stop in front of Cassie. "I think that's what worries me the most. What if he lies to me again? What if he's angry that I used his and my mother's DNA for the comparison? He didn't want me to do it." She shook her head. "This could explain why."

"No matter what, your father is your father. Give him the benefit of the doubt. Ask him for the truth."

Abby lifted the comparison chart and stared down at it. "I need to think about how to approach him. God, I hate this."

Cassie rose from her chair and wrapped her arms around Abby. "If you need me to come with you, I will."

She shook her head. "No, I have to confront him by myself. I don't want to put him on the spot in front of others."

"I'm here if you need me. Call, and I'll drop everything and come." She smoothed Abby's hair down her back. "I'm sure your father has a perfectly logical explanation."

Abby hugged Cassie. "Thank you. I don't know what I'd do without someone I can trust to talk to. I don't even have a mother I can go to." She stepped back. "We never had much of a connection. And she's been losing touch with reality for the past year. She wakes up screaming and telling me about her nightmares as if they were real."

"It must be terrifying to wake up every day and not know where you are or who the people around you are." Cassy pasted a soft smile on her face. "Things will work out, one way or another. Just know you have friends who are like family."

Abby nodded. "I'm not alone."

"Not at all. If you need a place to stay, you're always welcome at the ranch. You can stay as long as you like."

"Good to know," Abby said. "That's a distinct possibility if my father blows a gasket." She drew in a deep, shaky breath. "I'd better go. I have to work the night shift at the Blue Moose."

"And I need to close up." Cassie walked with Abby to the door and let her out. As she locked the door behind the younger woman, the desk phone rang.

Cassie hurried over to answer. "Eagle Rock Sheriff's Department, Deputy Douglas speaking."

"Oh, good. Just the person I needed to talk to. This is Preston Todd with the Montana State Crime Lab. We've completed our examination of the female you found entombed behind a wall. I'll send the full report via email, but we thought you might want the digest version sooner."

"Yes!" Cassie said, her heart racing. She sat at the desk and pulled out a pad and pen. "Tell me what you know."

"We estimate she was between twenty-six and thirty years old with blond hair. She died approximately twenty years ago."

"Cause of death?" Cassie asked.

"Fractured skull."

Cassie's heart constricted for the poor woman. "Blunt-force trauma?"

"We don't think so. It looked more like she'd had a fall where she hit her head on a sharp corner and suffered a brain bleed."

A blonde between twenty-six and thirty years old who'd died twenty years ago. Finally, she could narrow her search a little more.

"There's another fact we found interesting," Preston said.

When the medical examiner paused, Cassie prompted. "Which was?"

"The victim was wearing a maternity dress."

Cassie's brow dipped. "She wore a maternity dress?"

"Yes. We didn't note any signs of the baby. If she was pregnant, she must have had the baby before she died."

A woman didn't usually wear a maternity dress unless she was pregnant.

"We didn't find any sign of the baby on the woman or in the room where she was found. The label on the dress read handcrafted by Alice Carter. That may or may not be significant, but every detail could count."

"We'll look into the label," Cassie said. "If it was handcrafted, it might be from a local artisan."

"Like I said," the medical examiner continued, "a report will come your way in the next fifteen minutes. Let us know if you have any other questions, and good luck identifying her."

The medical examiner ended the call.

Cassie stared at the notes she'd taken, excited to get started with more filters to use in her sort.

Pregnant. That ought to narrow her search significantly.

She glanced at the clock on the wall. Almost six. Her date would be at the tavern by now. Cassie was supposed to meet Drake there for dinner rather than eat at the office for the third night straight.

With this new data, she couldn't walk away from the computer. This could be the breakthrough she'd been waiting for.

Cassie sent a text to Drake.

M.E.'s report is in. Staying at the office.

She didn't ask him to join her and wouldn't expect him to if he didn't want to.

A moment later, a text popped up on her screen. Be there in fifteen with dinner.

Cassie smiled. The man knew how important this case was to her and didn't begrudge her the time she needed to work through the data.

With a smile on her face and warmth in her heart for the Navy SEAL, Cassie dove into the databases with the information she desperately needed to narrow her search.

Twenty minutes later, a sharp knock sounded on the door in the front lobby.

Cassie leaped to her feet and ran to let Drake in. He carried a large bag filled with to-go boxes. The scents emitted made her belly rumble, reminding her she hadn't actually eaten lunch on her lunch break hours earlier.

She took the bag from him, leaned up on her toes and kissed Drake full on the lips. "You're a life-saver."

"You're cute." He cupped her cheek and deepened the kiss.

For a moment, Cassie forgot about the food, the data and the fact she was standing in the sheriff's office. The world faded away when they kissed.

When Drake lifted his head, the world rushed back in. Holding the big bag in one hand, she used her other to grab Drake's arm. "Come. Sit. I'll fill you in."

He followed her into the little office and pulled a chair up to the desk where she'd been working before dropping into it.

Cassie told him what she'd learned from the M.E. and showed him the search parameters she'd used on the Montana Missing Persons Database. "I'm going to start with Montana and then expand outward to a two-hundred-mile radius."

While Cassie worked over the computer, talking through what she was doing, Drake laid out the meal he'd brought.

The Montana-only search for a blond pregnant woman between the ages of twenty-six and thirty, who'd disappeared twenty years ago, came up empty.

"What if she had bleached her hair?" Drake suggested.

Cassie removed the filter of blond hair.

Five women came up.

Of the five, one was blond.

"I want to expand the search to a two-hundred-fifty-mile radius and add back the blond hair color. The medical examiner said she was blond. Surely, if she were a bleach blond, he would've seen the roots and noted it."

"That will take you into Idaho," Drake said

Cassie nodded, switched to the national missing

persons database, entered the filters and waited for the results.

The search brought up twenty women.

While picking at the club sandwich Drake had brought for her, Cassie read through the information on each female.

One woman from Cody, Wyoming, had been the mother of three small children. She'd been four months pregnant when she'd disappeared twenty years ago. The notes on her file indicated she'd been the victim of domestic violence, having called 911 on multiple occasions. Her husband had been arrested for beating her. When it came time to press charges, she'd refused to do it.

"Sounds like he either killed her," Drake said, "or she left to save her own life."

"Our victim wore a maternity dress, but there was no sign of a baby inside her," Cassie reminded him and herself. "She had to have been far enough along to deliver the baby before she died. And if she'd delivered it months before, she wouldn't have been wearing the maternity dress anymore."

"So, we're looking for a woman who was far enough along to wear a full-on maternity dress and who could've delivered shortly before she died."

Cassie nodded. "It's a lot of guessing, but it makes more sense."

They read through five more files. Each woman had been pregnant but not very far along. One had just found out she was pregnant, disappearing less than a week later.

They'd gone through seven of the women on the list of twenty.

"Am I being too restrictive?" Cassie asked.

"Let's get through the entire list before we answer that question." He gave her a teasing grin. "Focus, deputy," he said in his best bad-ass, military tone.

Cassie nodded and brought up the next woman.

"Who do we have this time," Drake asked.

Cassie read aloud. "Beth Anderson from Idaho Falls, Idaho. Twenty-seven years old. Not married. Eight and a half months pregnant when she disappeared. She left home in her car the morning she disappeared. Neither she nor her car were ever found."

Cassie stared into the compelling young face of a pretty blonde with blue eyes. Something about the woman tugged at Cassie.

"This one has potential," she said, writing Beth's name on her pad before moving on.

They went through the rest of the files. Most of the women weren't far along in their pregnancies.

After she closed the last file, she brought up the one that had been the closest to the data provided by the medical examiner.

Again, the face and eyes tugged at Cassie in a way none of the rest had. She picked up the telephone on the desktop.

"It's after normal work hours," Drake pointed out. "If you're calling the sheriff or police department, you should do it tomorrow morning when the people who handle files and cold cases are available."

Cassie frowned. "You're right. They'd have to dig out old case files. I'm certain the people in charge of those won't be there this late." She stared at the screen, frustrated that she'd have to wait until the morning to contact anyone.

"Can I?" Drake pulled the keyboard closer to him, brought up another screen and keyed in the names Scott and Amy Anderson Idaho Falls, Idaho.

"Her parents?" Cassie asked.

He nodded as a list popped up of various places on the internet where Scott and Amy were mentioned.

One of the places was a call to action, which the couple had posted over a year ago, asking anyone with information about their daughter Beth's disappearance to call them. Plus, their phone number had been listed below the request.

Cassie punched the numbers into the phone, held her breath and waited for it to ring. Her gaze met Drake's as the line rang and someone finally picked up.

"You have reached a special phone line set up by William and Amy Anderson. If you're calling with information about the disappearance of our daughter Beth Anderson, please leave your name, telephone number and a brief message. We'll get back to you as soon as possible."

"This is Deputy Cassie Douglas from Eagle Rock, Montana. I'd like to get more information about the disappearance of Beth Anderson. Please give me a call at…" Cassie left the number to the phone on the desk and ended the call. Her hand remained on the phone for a few seconds after placing it on the desk.

Drake covered her hand. "It's getting late. Whoever screens those calls probably won't get to it until tomorrow."

Cassie nodded. "You're right. I'm tired. Tomorrow's Friday, and I have the day off. I can pick up where we left off in the morning." She pushed to her feet and looked around the office. "You'd think I live here."

With Drake's help, she picked up the food containers and straightened the desk.

When they were finished, she switched off the light in the office and headed for the front door.

"I really need to do a better job of managing my expectations," she said.

"How so?" Drake asked as he opened the door.

"After banging my head against the wall all week, searching through thousands of cases, I thought what the M.E. would give us would be the magic bullet that could lead us straight to our victim's identity." She laughed. "The thing that kills me is that I know better."

"I wouldn't be so hard on myself," Drake said. "It's late. If you'd received that information earlier in the day, it might've been that magic bullet. Wait and see. Tomorrow might make all the difference."

She smiled up at him. "You're right. It's all about timing." Cassie leaned up to brush her lips across his. "And it's time to go back to your place. I feel the need to get physical."

Drake's eyes flared. His hand snaked around her waist and dragged her against him. "I can help with that."

"In the best possible way," she said.

As she crossed the threshold, the sound of a telephone ringing made her pause.

She glanced over her shoulder. "You think it could be…"

Drake stepped back. "You won't know unless you answer that call."

Cassie hurried back to the office, hit the light switch and snatched the phone off the desk. "Eagle Rock Sheriff's Department, this is Deputy Douglas. How can I help you?"

"Deputy Douglas, this is Amy Anderson. Did you just leave a message on the dedicated helpline we had set up to gather information concerning the disappearance of our daughter Beth?"

"Yes, ma'am." Cassie's gaze met Drake's as he entered the office. She put the phone on speaker so that he could hear the conversation as well. "Ma'am,

I'd like to ask some questions about your daughter's disappearance. Do you have a moment?"

For a long moment, Amy didn't respond.

"Mrs. Anderson?"

"I'm still here," she said, though her voice sounded choked. "If you want to ask questions, you'll have to come to our house in Idaho Falls when my husband is here."

"Ma'am, I'm in Eagle Rock, Montana. That's a four or five-hour drive."

"If you want to talk with us, it has to be in person. Too many pranksters have led us on wild goose chases. It's too hard."

"When will your husband be back?"

"He's in West Yellowstone, running his brother's campground while his brother and his wife are on vacation. He'll be back Monday night. I'm going up tomorrow to keep him company."

"Ma'am," Cassie said. "Would it be possible for me to meet with you and your husband in West Yellowstone tomorrow afternoon? It's at least an hour closer to me."

"I suppose," Amy said. "Only, please, don't come if you're trying to sell me something."

"I'm not trying to sell you something. I just want to understand your daughter's case a little better."

"Do you have any information about her?" she asked, her tone hopeful.

"Only what I've seen on the missing persons database."

Amy sighed. "Although it's been so long, I won't give up hope. Yes, my husband and I will meet with you tomorrow." She gave Cassie the address of the campground. They agreed on a time, and Cassie ended the call.

"I hate to get her hopes up," Cassie said.

"If our woman in the wall was her daughter, she'll want to know."

"If she's not," Cassie's lips pressed together in a thin line. "It'll be yet another disappointment and more heartache."

Drake held out his hand. "Ready to go?"

Cassie nodded. "I am. Especially if we go back to the plan."

"And what plan was that."

Cassie stepped close to him and laid her hand on his chest, drawing a line with her fingertip down the length of his torso to the waistband of his jeans. She lowered her voice to whisper, "Let's get out of here before I embarrass myself at my place of work. I could get fired if I act on what's going through my head right now."

Drake groaned. "Keep those thoughts." He grabbed her hand and marched her through the station and out the door.

Cassie turned to lock the door then followed Drake to his truck. Once they were both inside and seatbelts buckled, Drake took off for the bed and breakfast.

As far as Cassie was concerned, Drake couldn't get them there fast enough. He could break every damned speed limit, and she wouldn't give a damn.

# CHAPTER 11

THE DRIVE to West Yellowstone was over three hours and took them through beautiful country with spectacular views. Having grown up in Texas, Drake drank in the vistas, glad he'd decided to come to Montana.

He enjoyed talking with Cassie along the way, learning more about her, her brother and their lives growing up on a Montana cattle ranch.

He felt more comfortable with her than any other woman he'd ever met. She was like a best friend with the added benefit of being an amazing lover.

When they arrived in the resort town of West Yellowstone, he slowed. The campground was easy to find. Soon, he pulled up to the campground office and parked.

A woman with steely gray hair peered through the window. Moments later, she stepped out onto the porch with a man with dark blond hair laced with streaks of gray. Both wore deeply-etched frowns on their faces.

Drake dropped down from the truck to the ground and met Cassie at the front. Together, they approached the scowling couple.

"Mr. and Mrs. Anderson?" Cassie called out.

They nodded.

The woman said, "I'm Amy." She turned to the man beside her.

"William Anderson," he said, his voice terse, almost hostile.

"I'm Deputy Douglas, and this is Deputy Morgan. Could we sit?"

"Pardon us if we're a little belligerent," Amy said. "We've been through so much, and we still haven't found our Beth."

Cassie nodded. "I completely understand. I lost a friend recently. I won't give up hope, either."

For a long moment, the Andersons stood still, unmoving except for their eyes, taking in every detail of the strangers who'd come to stir them up over the daughter they hadn't seen in twenty years. Their wounds had never healed.

Mr. Anderson stepped back and waved toward the door. "You can come inside." He opened it and held it while his wife led the way inside to a table.

"Please, be seated," Mrs. Anderson said.

Drake held a chair for Cassie and waited for her to settle before claiming a seat for himself.

Mr. Anderson sat at the head of the table. Mrs. Anderson went behind the counter and returned with a heavy photo album, placing it on the table between Drake and Cassie.

"This is all we have left of our daughter, Beth," she said. "Pictures and memories. By now, we figure we'd be insane to believe she's still alive, but until we know for sure, that little bit of hope won't die."

Her husband patted the table beside him.

Amy sat, took a deep, steadying breath and folded her hands in her lap. Her pale blue gaze met Cassie's and held. "It's been twenty years. Why are you looking into my daughter's disappearance?"

Cassie looked from Amy to William and back. "Look, I could dance around the issue and come up with a plausible story short of the truth just to get you to open up, but I won't do that." She shot a glance toward Drake. "The truth is that we found a woman's body in an old lodge, and we're trying to identify her."

Amy covered her mouth with her hand, her eyes welling with tears. "And you think this…body might be our Beth?" Several fat teardrops rolled down Amy's cheeks.

William Anderson's eyes narrowed to slits. "You better have a good reason to believe it might be Beth and aren't just taking a shot in the dark. Every time someone comes to us saying they think they've found our daughter, it's like having another piece of your heart ripped from your chest. So, tell me what you know."

Drake gave a watered-down version of construction workers discovering the body in a secret room in the lodge. He didn't go into detail about the room being sealed with the woman inside.

"The Montana State Crime Lab determined the woman had blond hair, was somewhere between twenty-six and thirty years old and was found wearing a maternity dress."

Amy buried her face in her hands and sobbed.

William put an arm around his wife and looked across at Cassie. "Beth was pregnant. She was due to deliver within two weeks of her disappearance. My wife and I weren't happy about the fact she would be a single mother, raising her child alone, but we were excited to get to know our grandchild."

"I searched the missing persons database and came up with several blond-haired, pregnant women within a two-hundred and fifty-mile radius of Eagle Rock. None of them were as far along as Beth."

"Why is that important to you finding the woman's identity?" William asked.

Cassie met and held William's gaze. "We found the body, dressed in a maternity dress, but there was no baby. Right or wrong, we guessed she'd had that baby before she...died."

Amy turned her face into her husband's chest and sobbed more.

Willam cleared his throat. "You don't know that this body you found was our Beth."

"No, we don't," Cassie said. "To make sure, I'd like to collect something of Beth's that might have her DNA in it, like a hairbrush."

Amy shook her head and looked at Cassie through red-rimmed eyes. "All I brought with me was this photo album." She flipped it open to a page with a woman on it. The woman smiled, a hand resting on her swollen belly.

"That's Beth a month before she disappeared. Everything was on track with the baby's development. She was healthy and eager to meet her baby.

"Can you tell me something about the father?" Cassie asked.

William's mouth set in a tight line. "Not much. The bastard knocked her up and left town."

"Was he from around here?" Drake asked.

Amy shook her head. "Beth wouldn't tell us his name. She had her own apartment and worked as a waitress at the truck stop diner. The pay was terrible, but the tips were great. She'd moved out as soon as she graduated high school."

"We tried to get her to go to college, but she wanted nothing to do with it."

"Until she'd worked several years as a waitress," Amy added. "She was just finishing the last of her core courses when she met a man at the truck stop. She said he was a construction worker, but not just a construction worker. He had bigger dreams and was working toward them."

William snorted. "He was a dreamer with no substance. He made our girl fall in love with him. We asked her to bring him home for dinner."

Amy flipped another page in the photo album. "She said they had to work too many hours and wouldn't have any time off until they'd completed the hotel they were building across from the truck stop where Beth worked."

"Beth was happy enough for a while. We couldn't tell her anything. Couldn't warn her about men who use women. She was in love." William's lip curled into a sneer.

Amy stopped on a page with a picture of their daughter smiling while holding a fluffy puppy. "Then they finished the hotel, and he left." She ran her fingers across the photo as if she could still feel her daughter. "Beth came home that night. She'd finished her shift at the truck stop. The hotel construction was complete across the way, with only a cleanup crew left behind. The rest of the men had packed up and gone. She went to her apartment, expecting to find Roland there. He'd taken all his belongings and disappeared."

"He'd lied about his name and where he was from." William stared at the photo of Beth smiling.

"When she tried to find him, there was no Roland Sanders living in Lewiston, Washington."

"Beth was heartbroken," Amy said. "Then, two weeks after he'd left, she came to me crying. She hadn't had her cycle in a month, so she'd purchased an early pregnancy test at the drug store." Amy's voice caught.

William continued in a flat tone, "Beth was pregnant."

"We were going to be grandparents," Amy whispered, the devastation in her expression crushing the soul out of Drake.

William patted his wife's hand. "We wanted her to finish her degree and get a job that would support her and the baby. She agreed, gave up her apartment and moved back in with us."

"Everything seemed to be heading in the right direction. She'd had a sonogram. The doctor said she was having a girl," Amy smiled at the memory. "We set up the baby's room in pastel pink and yellow, bought a new crib and all the things it takes to raise a baby today. Beth seemed to be happier. Then, two weeks from her due date, she got into her car and drove to work. Or so we thought.

"When she didn't come home that night, we got worried and went to the truck stop. They said she'd handed in her resignation that morning. One of the waitresses said she'd told her that she was going to get the baby's daddy to cough up some child support for her daughter. She didn't say where she was going or how she'd found the man. She just got in her car and drove away.

"That was the last time anyone saw her," her mother said. "She didn't come back. We lost her that day and the granddaughter we were prepared to love as much as we loved Beth."

Amy flipped a couple more pages in the photo album and stopped on one of Beth, wearing a maternity dress in a pink and yellow floral print. She smiled into the camera while cupping her hands around the baby still nestled snuggly in her huge belly.

"We took this picture the week before she left. She was wearing that same dress the day she disappeared."

Drake's heart slipped to the bottom of his gut. Cassie reached for his hand and held on tightly, her face pale, the fine lines around her lips and eyes digging deeper.

"Mrs. Anderson, who made that dress?" Cassie asked slowly, her words measured and clear.

"I had it handmade by a local fabric artist, Alice Carter. It's one of a kind. Beth loved it so much. She was cool and comfortable in it, especially the further along she got."

Drake exchanged a glance with Cassie. She gave him an almost imperceptible nod.

"What?" William's gaze darted from Cassie to Drake.

"The maternity dress the victim wore was made by Alice Carter and had little pink and yellow flowers on it."

Amy's eyes widened.

William countered, "I'm sure this Alice Carter woman made more dresses with that fabric than just the one she made for Beth."

His wife sat beside him shaking her head. "It was the only one. She swore." Amy's eyes filled again. "You found Beth."

CASSIE STARED at the road ahead, her mind too drained to make conversation. An hour and a half passed before she turned to Drake.

"I thought learning the victim's name would make me feel better." She shook her head. "Seeing the fresh shock and overwhelming sorrow in Amy and William Anderson's faces broke my heart. No one should outlive their child."

"I agree," Drake said. "You could tell they wanted to believe she was still alive."

"I told them they could ask for a DNA test to prove she's their daughter."

"Do you have any doubts?" Drake asked

Cassie shook her head. "It has to be Beth. It can't

be a coincidence that she was wearing a one-of-a-kind maternity dress with that specific pattern."

"I'm glad they didn't see her the way I found her," Drake said.

Cassie touched his arm. "It makes it all too real, seeing her photographs when she was alive and listening to her parents talk about her. They loved her so much."

Drake glanced toward her. "Did you forward the snapshot you took of Beth wearing the dress to the state crime lab?"

Cassie nodded. "I got a response from Preston Todd. The patterns matched. They'll be in touch with the Andersons so they can make arrangements to transfer Beth's body to Idaho Falls, where she'll be buried among family."

Drake nodded. "She'll finally get to go home."

"And her parents will have the closure they needed." Cassie prayed she wouldn't have to wait twenty years to find Penny. "This case isn't over yet," Cassie said. "We have to find out who murdered Beth and sealed her in the wall."

"The Andersons said the father of Beth's child was in construction." Drake glanced toward Cassie.

Cassie nodded. "It can't be a coincidence that she found her way to Eagle Rock and ended up sealed into a wall during a construction project. One of the men working for Greenway Construction had to have done it. Or someone who had access to the construction site."

"It had to be someone at Greenway," Drake said. "Why else kill Earl? Earl might've known who else was hanging drywall beside himself."

"You and the sheriff interviewed all the workers who still live nearby." Cassie frowned. "Nothing?"

"I can't vouch for the men Sheriff Barron spoke with. I didn't get any guilty vibes from the ones I contacted, but then, one of them might be a really good liar."

"He convinced Beth he was sincere," Cassie pointed out.

Drake nodded.

The road heading into the Crazy Mountains narrowed on each side and curved between sheer bluffs.

Drake's hands tightened on the steering wheel as he navigated the switchbacks.

"You might want to slow down even more," Cassie cautioned. "These roads can be just as treacherous even during good driving conditions."

"We don't have curves like this in Texas," Drake said. "Nor do we have mountains this high or steep. Does this road ever get cut off in the winter?"

Cassie nodded. "There have been occasions when avalanches claim sections of the highway. Other roads lead in and out of the mountains, but this highway is the more direct route to Bozeman. Avalanche control units will set off charges to trigger smaller avalanches to keep the big ones from happening. In the winter, you might hear the explosions after a heavy snowfall."

"We don't have those in Texas, either." Drake grinned and lowered his window.

Cassie enjoyed her view of Drake taking in the beauty of the Crazy Mountains. "Do you like it here in Montana?"

Drake nodded. "I love it."

"Even with dead women and mechanics turning up?" she asked.

With his gaze firmly fixed on the curves, he said. "We have drive-by shootings in Houston and discontented teens attacking schools. We don't have the Rocky Mountains with views to die for."

A loud boom echoed off the sides of the mountains they were passing through.

Cassie frowned. "Did you hear that?"

Drake laughed. "Hard not to hear that. What was it?"

"Sounded just like the charges they use to manage avalanches. Only it isn't something you hear in the summer."

A rumbling sound followed, building in intensity and shaking Drake's truck as he rounded a tight curve and slammed on the brakes.

Barely ten feet in front of them, tons of gravel,

rocks, boulders and tree trunks slid down a steep slope.

"Holy shit." Cassie shot a glance up the hill and yelled, "Back up!"

The landslide was widening. If Drake didn't move quickly, it would take out the section of road where his truck stood and twenty yards behind him.

Drake slammed the shift into reverse and punched the accelerator.

They made it fifteen feet to the rear before the landslide caught up with them and swept the truck off the road and downward.

Cassie held on to the oh-shit handle above the door and prayed the truck didn't roll or get swallowed by the crushing force of rocks, gravel and boulders.

The roar was deafening as the side of the mountain continued to slide to the bottom of the hill.

Drake reached out his hand and captured Cassie's free one. "In case we don't make it out of this alive... I'm falling in love with you!"

Cassie could barely distinguish his words over the mind-numbing sounds. But if she heard him right, he'd just admitted to falling in love with her.

Her heart swelled at the same time as anger burned inside. "Damn it, Drake! You don't tell a girl you love her when you're both about to die!"

"Quit cussing me and tell me you love me, too!"

"You're ridiculous!" she shouted. "And despite it all, I love you, too. We damn well better not die."

The truck rocked, lurched and tipped several times precariously, more or less surfing the wave of earth slipping into the valley below. Boulders pressed against the side panels, screeching across the metal, adding to the thunder of the landslide.

Cassie held onto Drake's hand with a grip that defied death as the truck seemed to be consumed by rock, gravel and boulders, slowly rising up the sides, almost to the windows. If the truck sank deeper, the flow of rocks and gravel would crush the windows and fill the cab like water in a sinking ship.

Cassie clutched Drake's hand and the oh-shit handle and prayed for a miracle.

# CHAPTER 12

JUST WHEN DRAKE thought the truck would collapse under the pressure of the landslide consuming it, the slope leveled out. Their descent slowed until they shuddered to a stop. Dust swam in the air inside the cab, but the rocks and gravel hadn't crushed the windows and filled the truck like grain pumped into a grain elevator.

The roar dissipated with residual rumbles. Compared to what it had been, it was now eerily quiet.

Drake glanced over at Cassie. "Are you all right?"

"Yes." She coughed and pulled the collar of her blouse over her nose. "Now what?"

"We get out of here before it gets dark and before another landslide finishes us off." He fished his cell phone out of his pocket and checked the reception bars.

"We never have reception in this area," she said.

"We won't be able to call for help." He slipped his phone back into his pocket.

"All the more reason to get out of here and back up to the highway before dark. I told my brother and Sheriff Barron where we were going and when we expected to get back. Hopefully, they'll come looking for us when we don't return in time. And if they find out there was an avalanche, they might get out here even sooner."

"Good thinking," Drake said. "My guys got the same briefing. Between all of them, someone should come looking for us."

"It might take them a while when they have to go around the mountain to get to us." She frowned and unbuckled her seatbelt. "Not to be a downer, but we also need to be watching for bears. It would be best if we don't have to stay the night in the open."

"No pressure," Drake said, feeling the pressure of their situation like the crushed side panels of his truck.

He pressed the button to lower the windows. They shimmied but didn't go down, probably due to being blocked by the crushed side panels.

He dug in the console for the emergency escape tool he'd never expected to use but had been smart enough to equip his truck with anyway. The tiny, pointy hammer didn't seem like it could do much. He placed the point against the window, and then smacked it sharply.

The window cracked where the point hit but didn't shatter as it had in the demonstration videos.

Then he remembered. "These don't work on tempered glass."

"I take it your window is tempered glass?" Cassie shook her head and pressed the button to lower her window. It went down halfway.

"I think I can get out." She looked at Drake and back at the narrow gap. "Sweetie, you're not getting through that."

His eyes narrowed, and his jaw firmed. "Watch me."

He had Cassie climb into the back seat. Then he sat on the console and kicked the slightly lowered window with both feet.

The first kick cracked the window slightly. The second expanded the crack.

Knowing they had little spare time to get back up the hill and go for help, he channeled all his energy into one more kick. When his booted heels hit the window, the tempered glass cracked at the bottom and flopped over as one cracked but intact piece.

Drake crawled through first, planted his feet firmly in the gravel and reached through the window for Cassie.

She wrapped her arms around his neck and let him pull her free of the truck.

His feet slipped in the loose gravel, and they both fell and slid further down the hill before they could get their feet beneath them.

"We need to get off the loose stuff," Drake said. "We don't want to get caught in it if it starts sliding again." He grabbed her hand and walked, slipped and skidded across the rocks and loose gravel until they reached a side where the avalanche hadn't spread over the landscape.

Cassie glanced up and whistled. "Wow. That's a long way up, and it's super steep."

Drake nodded. "I'd say stay here until I can get help, but I can't leave you to another moving hillside or killer bears." Still holding her hand, he started up the steep incline, grabbing saplings and tree roots to steady himself and pull himself and Cassie up the steepest areas.

Halfway up, his muscles and lungs burned from the effort. With the sun slipping quickly behind the highest mountain peak, they didn't have time to stop for a break.

He pushed upward, not wanting to be caught on the steep slope in the dark. If one or both of them fell, they could be injured, and no one would find them until the morning, if at all.

By the time he reached the top, his arms and legs shook. He turned and pulled Cassie up over the edge and onto the pavement.

They collapsed side by side and lay for several

minutes, catching their breath and giving their muscles a break from the strenuous climb.

"As nice as it is to lie beside you," Cassie said. "I'd rather we were on a soft bed."

"We can arrange that," he said. Pushing to his feet, he reached down and dragged Cassie into his arms and kissed her long and hard.

Then he stood beside her, looking down the steep incline at the river of rock and gravel that had consumed a major portion of the highway and Drake's pickup.

"That could've played out a lot worse," he said.

Cassie nodded and slipped an arm around his waist. "I meant what I said as we were plummeting to our deaths. It wasn't just an only-because-we're-going-to-die sentiment. For some dumb reason, you've found your way firmly beneath my skin. Now, if you decide you spoke too soon and in the heat of the moment, I won't hold you to what you said." She knew she was rattling on but couldn't find a way to stop, even when Drake turned her to face him.

"People sometimes say things in the heat of the moment that they don't really mean. We were pretty much in the heat of the moment. Nothing should count if that's the way you want to go."

Drake touched a finger to her lips. "However, I meant what I said. I didn't mean for it to happen, and definitely not so quickly. I can't unlike you or pretend I don't care in order to satisfy some arbitrary grace period we're supposed to wait through before we can believe what we've felt all along is real."

"I never knew what love was…"

"Until you," Drake said at the same time as Cassie.

They laughed, held each other and kissed.

Once the sun dipped completely below the peaks, darkness descended, and the temperature dropped. Starlight competed with the shadows cast by the mountains, making it almost impossible to see the road in front of them.

They walked back the way they'd come, having no other choice with the road washed out by a river of rock.

The road Drake had zigzagged through the mountains seemed to wind around forever. When he thought it would never end, they emerged into a valley where the starlight helped illuminate their way.

"There should be a house near here," Cassie said. "I know this valley. I've passed through this area so many times throughout my life. Funny how I never noticed the homes here."

"Hopefully, one will have a landline phone we can use to call for someone to come get us."

A light shone in the distance from a security lamp perched high on a pole. Hope gave them a little more energy, and they picked up their pace.

They'd gone halfway across the valley when the

thumping sound of rotors beating the air echoed off the surrounding hillsides.

A helicopter popped up over a peak and swooped into the valley, shining a high-powered spotlight. Eventually, the spotlight found them.

The chopper hovered overhead for a moment, then landed on the road thirty yards from where Drake and Cassie stood.

A tall figure emerged from the helicopter and strode toward them.

As the man neared, Drake recognized Hank Patterson.

The first words out of Hank's mouth were, "Thank God." He held out a hand to Drake.

When Drake gripped him, Hank pulled him into a hug. "We thought you two were caught in the landslide."

"We were," Cassie said

Hank released Drake and enveloped Cassie in another heartfelt hug.

"What do you mean you were caught in the land-slide?" He held Cassie at arm's length. "Were you hurt?"

She shook her head.

"Thankfully, we survived," Drake said. "The same can't be said for my truck. We were carried to the bottom of a steep hill where the landslide spread out and slowed to a stop."

"I'm just glad you're okay." Hank led the way to

the helicopter, helped Cassie up into the back and buckled the safety harness around her. Drake settled on the seat beside her and buckled up. Hank climbed into the co-pilot's seat and slipped a headset over his ears.

Within moments, the helicopter lifted off the ground, rising straight up to clear the peaks, and headed northeast toward Eagle Rock.

When they could see the lights from Eagle Rock, the chopper slowed. A few miles short of town, it landed on a designated pad on a sprawling ranch.

Hank climbed out of the co-pilot's seat and helped Cassie down from the helicopter.

Once Hank, Drake and Cassie were on the ground, the chopper rose and disappeared into the night sky.

"Come," Hank said. "It's getting late, but I'm almost certain Sadie will be awake, fixing lemonade, sweet tea and whiskey."

"I could use some of that whiskey," Cassie said.

"You two are welcome to stay the night," Hank said. "In fact, after what you've been through, it would be better all around. And it's late; you don't want to wake Ms. Dottie at the B&B."

Drake nodded. "Thank you."

Hank smiled. "Don't worry. We'll find some clothes for you both so you can shower off the dust."

As Hank had predicted, his wife Sadie was

waiting for them when they entered the beautiful, sprawling home.

She had a tray prepared on the kitchen bar with food and drinks.

"You two must be exhausted. I have rooms ready for you. Get something to eat and drink, and I'll take you up." She walked into Hank's arms and kissed him soundly. "I don't like it when you go up in the helicopter at night. I'm always afraid you'll crash into a mountain."

"My pilot knows what he's doing. Besides, we found Drake and Cassie alive. None of us were sure we would."

"Did you notify Cassie's brother and Sheriff Barron?"

Hank nodded. "And we let Molly McKinnon and the crew Drake's been working with know he made it back safe and not to expect him at the B&B tonight." He kissed the top of her blond hair. "Did I get everybody?"

She laughed. "I think so." She turned to Drake and Cassie. "A lot of people were worried about you. Even Abby Matson called the sheriff asking where you were."

Cassie frowned. "What time is it?"

"Past midnight," Sadie said. "Please, eat something."

Drake snagged a roast beef sandwich from the stack of sandwiches and polished it off quickly. He hadn't realized how hungry he was. They'd planned on eating supper once they got back to Eagle Rock, never suspecting they would be four hours later than planned—and lucky to be there at all.

Cassie nibbled at the cheese cubes and olives, washing them down with lemonade. After a few bites, she brushed the crumbs from her fingers.

"Do you know if anyone is doing avalanche control this time of year?" Cassie asked.

Hank frowned. "They don't do that until there's a lot of snow in the mountains. Why?"

"Before the landslide, we heard what sounded like the canons they shoot off to trigger the snow to fall."

"I can't imagine anyone doing that during the summer," Hank said. "You think that triggered the landslide?"

"Pretty sure," Cassie said. "We ran into the landslide immediately following the boom."

"I'll have my computer guy, Swede, check into it."

"If you're finished," Sadie said, "I'll show you where you can shower and sleep."

Sadie led the way up a curved staircase to the second floor. Passing a few doors, she stopped in front of one of the rooms and pushed open the door. "Cassie, I put you in here. The bed is soft, and you have your own shower. I'll come back by with some night clothes."

Leaving Cassie in her room, Sadie led the way to the next room, threw open the door and waved

Drake through it. "You have a shower and clean towels. If you need anything else, let me know. I'm glad you and Cassie made it out of that landslide intact. I'm sure it was frightening."

Drake thanked her and waited for Sadie's footsteps to retreat before he stepped back out into the hallway and knocked softly on Cassie's door.

She pulled it open, grabbed his shirt and dragged him across the threshold and into her arms.

Drake stripped out of his dusty clothes and helped Cassie out of hers. Together, they slipped into the shower and washed each other's bodies until their skin glowed and they were ready to take the action to the bedroom.

After a quick rubdown with towels, Drake scooped Cassie up in his arms, carried her into the bedroom and laid her across the bed.

He dropped onto the mattress beside her and held her for a long moment.

She cupped his cheek and pressed her lips to his. "We nearly died today, and all I could think was, I'm not ready for this to end."

His heart swelled. "I had the same thought. I'd finally found someone who fit me like she was the other half of my heart. Cassie, you make me feel complete. You're gutsy, caring, smart and beautiful. I want to love you until we're old and gray and beyond."

She smiled. "You say it better than I ever could. I

love that you're strong and capable and that you recognize I can be, too, without it threatening your masculinity. You care enough about a woman you never met to want to help her family find peace. And you love me for me, not for the person you want me to be. Hell, I'm not a poet." She pressed her lips to his. "I just love everything about you."

He laughed and held her close. "It's enough."

She leaned close and whispered into his ear, "Now, shut up and make love to me."

He'd been exhausted by the long day driving to Idaho and back, the terror of nearly being crushed to death by a landslide and the harrowing climb up the side of the mountain. But her words and the way her body moved against his sparked flames inside him. Adrenaline moved blood through his veins, providing the burst of energy he needed to bring her to the edge and beyond.

He touched and tasted every inch of her body, stroking the places that brought her the greatest pleasure. She cried out his name and clung to him, her body pulsing with her release.

Then she urged him to take her.

"Please," she begged.

Drake leaned over the side of the bed, snagged his jeans, and pulled his wallet from the back pocket. Thankfully, he'd restocked the day before. With the little foil packet in hand, he rolled back into the bed.

Cassie took control of the packet, tore it open and

rolled the condom over his shaft, her hands lingering at the base, fondling him, making him even harder.

Then she guided him to her entrance and brought him home.

They settled into a rhythm, him pressing into her, her rocking her hips to meet his every thrust. The pace increased with their need until the tension built to the ultimate climax.

Drake thrust one last time, going deep.

Cassie locked her legs around him, holding him there as waves of sensation washed him ashore.

He collapsed onto her, breathing hard. Then he rolled over, taking her with him, holding her close as his heart rate slowly returned to normal.

Yeah, they still had a killer to find, one who might be getting desperate to keep his identity secret. Drake suspected the avalanche hadn't been an act of nature but rather an attempt on Drake and Cassie's lives for getting too close to the truth. Danger was knocking on their door, but, for that moment, all Drake wanted was right here in his arms.

He fell asleep with Cassie's body pressed to his, thankful for another day with the woman who had so quickly become his life.

# CHAPTER 13

CASSIE WOKE to sunlight streaming through the window, filling the room with a happy glow that made her want to embrace the day.

The sense of joy was compounded as a muscular arm tightened around her, pulling her close to the man to whom she'd given her heart.

Having almost died the day before, the terror of being swept down a mountainside in a sea of rock and boulders seemed almost inconsequential in comparison to the fear of falling in love again. Yet, here she was, in his arms, loving and being loved by a man so special she didn't know what she'd done to deserve him.

"Good morning, beautiful," he said, his voice deep and rumbly.

"Good morning," she said, turning over to snuggle

in his arms. "I wish we could hide in this room for a couple of days."

He nodded and tightened his hold. "Me, too."

"But we're not on a deserted island. We're in Hank and Sadie's house, and we'll be expected to join them for breakfast and fill them in on what we learned in Idaho." She sighed.

"Or we can stay in this bed and make love until they come banging on the door to kick us out for making too much noise." He nuzzled her neck, his hands smoothing down her naked back to cup her ass.

"Mmm. I like the way you think." She slid her calf up to his thigh.

His cock grew and hardened against her belly.

Cassie rolled him onto his back and straddled him, poised to take him into her and ride him like the stud he was.

He gripped her hips and stopped her short. "Protection?"

Her eyes rounded. She'd almost forgotten in her mind-number desire. "Your wallet?"

He shook his head. "We used the only one I had last night."

"Can't you just withdraw at the last second?"

"Sweetheart, when we're ready to talk children, I want it to be a deliberate decision, not an accident of lust. I want you to want me for me and not be in this relationship because you feel you have to for the sake of a child."

Cassie sighed. "I hate it when you're so logical."

"And I love that you're on top." He slapped her ass playfully. "Save it for tonight when we have what we need."

"Deal." She leaned forward, kissed him hard on the mouth, and then rolled off the bed onto her feet. "Let's make the most of this day. I feel we're so close to solving this case that today might be the day."

A knock sounded on the door.

"Cassie," Sadie's voice sounded through the panel. "I brought you clothes I think you can wear for the day. I'll leave them outside your door. And Hank found some for Drake, too. I have breakfast started but take your time. Don't feel like you have to hurry."

Cassie's gaze met Drake's as they stood on the other side of the door from Sadie, completely naked. A giggle rose in her throat. She covered her mouth and waited for the sound of Sadie's footsteps to recede.

Drake grabbed Cassie around the waist and rolled her onto the bed. "You heard the woman…take your time."

Cassie laughed and pressed her body against his. She loved being skin to skin with him. "Nothing would give me more pleasure than to lie here all day with you."

"With an unlimited supply of condoms," he kissed her long and hard then got up. He held out his hand. "Come on, woman. We have a killer to catch."

She laid her hand in his and let him draw her to her feet, her lips twisting into a wry grin. "You know how to sweep a woman back onto her feet."

He grinned. "Just keeping it real." Drake crossed to the door and opened it wide enough to grab the piles of clothing left there.

After closing the door, he carried the items into the bathroom and switched on the shower.

They got in together and lathered soap all over the other's body. Cassie's hands lingered on Drake's engorged shaft.

"You're making this harder than it has to be," Drake grumbled.

She laughed. "No kidding. But we can fix that." Cassie reached behind him and turned the faucet handle to cold. Then she jumped out of the shower, laughing as he swore.

Toweling dry was just as much fun, taking longer than it should have.

By the time they were dressed, their hair combed and shoes on, Cassie could smell bacon.

Her stomach rumbled.

They descended the steps hand in hand and followed the yummy smells to the kitchen, where Hank manned the skillet with the bacon, Sadie stirred fluffy yellow eggs in another pan and two children played with wooden spoons and plastic mixing bowls on the floor.

Cassie's chest tightened at the scene of this beautiful family making breakfast together. She realized she wanted that. If what they had continued to be as good as it felt now, could this be them in a few years? The idea was scary, exciting and desired.

Cassie and Drake helped set the table and pour orange juice into glasses and coffee into mugs. Hank laid platters of bacon and toast on the table and went back to the stove to collect another Sadie had filled with scrambled eggs.

Sadie lifted their dark-haired little boy from the floor and fitted him into a highchair while Hank helped the golden-haired little girl into a booster seat at the table.

Everyone took a seat and helped themselves to the food.

While they ate, Cassie and Drake filled Hank in on what they'd learned in Idaho, careful about what they said in front of the little ones.

"I'll double-check with Margaret and find out if Greenway Construction did work in Idaho Falls twenty years ago," Cassie said.

"It had to be Greenway," Drake said. "Why else would a heavily pregnant Beth Anderson come all the way to Eagle Rock, Montana?"

"Margaret might also know who worked the job

in Idaho." Cassie's gaze met Drake's. "It could've been a smaller subset of the crew working the Lucky Lady Lodge addition."

Sadie smiled as she pushed to her feet and started collecting plates. "Sounds like you two have your day lined up."

"Let us know if we can be of assistance." Hank stood and helped his wife. "And if you have time and want to come back out here, we're having a barbecue tonight for the Brotherhood Protectors and the crew of spec ops folks working on the lodge's renovations."

"Thank you." Cassie drank the last of her orange juice and pushed to her feet. "You two have been too kind." She grinned. "And I love the outfit."

Sadie smiled. "You can keep it. It was one of the outfits from the movie we made last year."

Cassie shook her head. "You're both so amazing. I don't know how you juggle your lives between movies, the Brotherhood and your beautiful children."

Hank slipped an arm around Sadie and dropped a kiss on top of her golden-blond hair. "We love each other enough to make it work."

"Don't get us wrong," Sadie said. "It's not always easy."

Hank stared into his wife's beautiful face. "But it's worth it."

Drake carried his dishes to the sink and rinsed

them before placing them in the dishwasher. "Whatever you're doing is working, and we really appreciate what you did for us last night." He turned with a grin. "It was almost like old times and made my heart proud when that helicopter came over the ridge and landed in front of us."

"I'm lucky to have a great support system in Eagle Rock and Bozeman. We have access to planes and helicopters when we need them."

"You're making a good sales pitch for coming to work for Brotherhood Protectors," Drake said.

Hank held up his hand. "Not pitching. Just stating the facts. You committed to helping Molly and Parker for the duration of the lodge renovation. When that's done, you'll be hearing the official sales pitch."

"We hate to eat and run," Cassie said, "but I feel like we're really close to finding out who was behind Beth Anderson and Earl Hensley's murders."

"And possibly behind the explosion that triggered the landslide that almost killed the two of you," Hank added. "They have to be connected. I don't believe in coincidence." Hank dug in his pocket and pulled out a set of keys. "Take my truck since yours was buried in the avalanche." He tossed the keys to Drake.

Drake caught them with one hand. "Thank you, Hank and Sadie. We hope to see you this evening if things work out."

Cassie hurried out the front door and into Hank's truck, anxious to get started.

Drake slipped into the driver's seat and started the engine.

"I feel on edge," Cassie said.

Drake shot a glance in her direction as he turned the truck around. "Like we're on the verge of cracking this case?"

"Yes. I'm eager to get to the truth and, at the same time, apprehensive."

Drake nodded. "Whoever we're dealing with has killed and tried to kill us in that avalanche. We're getting close, and it's making him nervous."

Cassie laughed. "Me, too."

"Where to first?" Drake asked. "Margaret's place or the sheriff's office?"

"Sheriff's office," Cassie said. "I need to check in and see if he's heard anything more from the M.E., and we need to tell him what we learned in Idaho."

"You left your vehicle there, right?"

"I did," she said.

"If it's all right with you, I'll leave you with the sheriff and let you give him the updates while I run out to talk to Margaret."

Cassie nodded. "Sounds good. I'll have my vehicle if I need to go anywhere or if we need to meet somewhere."

As they drove into Eagle Rock, it looked the same

as it did every day to Cassie. But it felt different. So much had happened in the past week. So many revelations. The small town she'd known all her life held secrets she'd never expected.

Drake pulled into the parking lot in front of the sheriff's office.

"Good, the sheriff is in," Cassie said as she unbuckled her seatbelt and climbed down from the truck. "See you in a few," she said with a wave and entered the building.

"Deputy Douglas...Cassie." Sheriff Barron crossed the room and pulled her into a crushing hug. "Woman, you scared the life out of me last night."

She laughed. "You can't possibly be as terrified as I was as we were swept down the hill in that avalanche."

The sheriff set her at arm's length, his gaze raking over her. "Have you been to see a doctor? Are you hurt?"

"I'm fine other than a few bruises. Drake's truck is toast. Buried to the windows in the half of the mountain that slipped down that hill." She studied her boss.

The man actually had tears in his eyes.

"I'm okay," she assured him. "I lived to work another day. You won't be stuck manning all the shifts."

"Shifts be damned. It's you I was worried about. This case is getting too dangerous. I'd pull you off it if I thought that would keep you out of trouble."

Cassie shook her head. "You can't pull me. We're getting too close to the answers. We know who the victim is. Now, we need to nail her killer."

"The fact that you're getting close is what has me scared and has the killer worried. I don't want what happened to Earl to happen to you." He gripped her arms. "And it almost did. That avalanche happened on purpose. I've heard from a number of sources that they heard a cannon go off right before the landslide."

"We heard it, too," Cassie said. "And I believe it was aimed at us." She lifted her chin. "All the more reason to push to the finish. He's scared and trying to keep people from knowing the truth. His actions are going to get him caught."

The sheriff's eyebrows formed a V over his nose. "Let's catch him before he claims another victim. I don't want the next victim to be you."

Cassie's heart warmed at the sheriff's words. The man had taken her under his wing after her parents' passing. He'd given her a job as a deputy and put her through the training, knowing she might eventually go back to law school and finish her degree. He wanted her to be successful, even if it wasn't with the sheriff's department.

He cared.

"Come into my office and tell me everything you got from your exciting trip to Idaho."

The sheriff settled behind his desk, and Cassie sat

in one of the chairs in front of him. In the next fifteen minutes, she told him everything they'd learned about Beth Anderson and her love affair with a construction worker.

When she finished, Sheriff Barron shook his head. "Her life was cut way too short. So, let me get this straight...she was eight and a half months pregnant when she disappeared from Idaho Falls. Seems to me we still need to solve two riddles—who the killer is and what happened to Beth's baby."

Cassie nodded. "Drake's on his way out to Margaret's to see if she remembers a Greenway Construction project in Idaho Falls. If so, we hope she can remember who worked on that project."

The sheriff's frown deepened. "Margaret came by the office yesterday and said she was afraid to stay at her house because she'd been getting too many threats."

"Damn," Cassie pulled her cell phone out of her pocket. "Do you know where she is?"

Sheriff Barron nodded. "I do. I sent her to my fishing shack with a cooler full of beer and snacks, a fishing pole and bait." He grinned. "She was pleased to go. Said fishing relaxed her, even if she didn't catch anything."

"Can you shoot the location to Drake on his cell phone?" Cassie asked. "We really need the information only she can provide." She sent Drake's cell phone number to the sheriff's phone.

Moments later, the sheriff had Drake on his way out to where Margaret would be happily fishing.

The sheriff's cell phone buzzed in his hand, and he lifted it to his ear. "Sheriff Barron speaking. Hello, Marnie. Whatcha got?"

Cassie watched the man's expression as he listened. Halfway through Marnie's message, he shook his head, indicating it had nothing to do with the case Cassie was working.

"Tell her I'll be there as soon as possible. Thank you, Marnie." The sheriff ended the call and gave Cassie a crooked grin. "Someone took Mrs. Crabtree's Cadillac for a joy ride last night. She wants me to dust for fingerprints and arrest the kids who did it." He sighed. "I'll be back as soon as possible."

Cassie shook her head. "Never a dull moment in Eagle Rock."

"I could use a few dull moments," the sheriff said as he left the building.

Intent on joining Drake out at Sheriff Barron's fishing shack to interview Margaret, she left the building and turned to lock the front door.

Cassie's cell phone rang in her pocket. She dug it out and noted Abby Matson's name on the display. She answered, "Hey, Abby, how's it going?"

"Not good," Abby said, her voice catching on what sounded like a sob. "Can you come to my house? I need you to come now."

"Are you okay?" Cassie ran for her car with the phone pressed to her ear.

"I'm okay," Abby said. "But Mom—Linda isn't."

Cassie jumped into her SUV and started the engine while trying to hold the phone to her ear. "Where's your father?"

"I don't know. He didn't come home last night. Cassie, he was so angry."

"You asked him about the DNA results?" Cassie pulled out of the parking lot and onto Main Street, heading north. Abby lived with her father and Linda two miles north of Eagle Rock on a five-acre tract of land. Frank had built a four-thousand-square-foot house on a hill with views of the Crazy Mountains in his backyard.

Cassie had never been inside the home, but she'd passed by it often. The stately structure on the hill rose above the trees surrounding the base.

Less than five minutes from leaving the sheriff's office, Cassie drove up the concrete driveway, parked beside the home and ran toward the front entrance.

Abby burst through the front door and ran down the porch steps, her eyes rid-rimmed, her hair in disarray. She flung herself into Cassie's arms and shook with the force of her sobs. "She's lost it. Linda's completely lost it. And she's got a gun."

Cassie stiffened and moved Abby to arm's length. "Where is she?"

"In the living room. She's smashing everything. I

tried to get her to stop, but she smashed the front of the gun cabinet and took out one of the handguns."

"Do you know if it's loaded?" Cassie asked, moving Abby to the corner of the house, out of sight of the living room windows.

"It wasn't, but she found the drawer with the bullets. I tried to reason with her. I even knocked the box of bullets from her hand, but she wouldn't listen. She yelled at me to leave her alone. She said I wasn't her daughter and never was, and if I didn't get the hell out of the house, she'd kill me like she killed her."

Cassie's gut clenched. "Did she say who she killed?"

"No, but she said she should've killed me when she killed her."

"Sweet Jesus," Cassie murmured. "The baby."

Abby gripped Cassie's arms. "What did she mean?"

"I'm not exactly sure." Cassie tried to pry Abby's fingers from her arms. "You need to let me handle this."

"No. You know something. What is it?" Abby's voice rose, her eyes wild. "If Linda isn't my mother, who is? You know, don't you? Did Linda kill my mother? Is that it? Linda killed my mother and raised me as her own? I should've known. I should've fucking known." Abby spun away, burying her face in her hands. "No wonder she hated my father and me."

Shots rang out from inside the house.

Cassie grabbed Abby, dragged her to the other side of her vehicle and pushed her to the ground. "Stay down. I'm going to see if I can disarm her."

Abby's fingers clutched at Cassie's arm. "No. Don't go in there. She's crazy. She'll kill you."

Cassie removed Abby's hand from her arm. "She's not going to kill me." At least Cassie hoped she wouldn't. "We can't help her until the gun is out of her hands. If you want to help me, do so by staying low and out of range. I need to worry about Linda. I can't do that if I'm worried about you."

Abby's eyes filled. "But if she shoots you…"

"I'll be okay."

"You're the only person I can talk to. My only friend. Please," she begged, "don't die."

Cassie squeezed Abby's hands. "I'm not going to die. But I need you to promise to stay here."

Another shot rang out.

Cassie ducked instinctively. "Promise," she commanded.

Abby nodded. "I promise."

Cassie didn't waste any more time. She left Abby behind her SUV, circled the house and entered through the kitchen door in the back.

Moving silently through the corridors, she followed the sound of glass breaking and loud curses. Another shot was fired, followed by two more.

Cassie hunkered down, moving carefully through the house toward the front living room.

She paused near the entrance, dropped low and peeked around the corner.

Linda Matson stood in the middle of the room, waving a handgun at the portrait hanging over the fireplace mantel. "One happy fucking family," she bit out. She aimed the gun at the portrait and pulled the trigger. "It's a lie. A big, fat, fucking lie!"

The woman's back was to Cassie.

As she raised her arm to aim at the portrait again, Cassie moved quickly and silently into the room and hit Linda from behind, sending her sprawling forward. The gun flew from her fingers and skidded to a corner, spinning to a stop.

Before Linda could get up, Cassie flung herself onto the woman and pinned her to the ground.

"Get off me!" Linda bucked with surprising strength, rolling Cassie to one side.

Cassie lurched to her feet at the same time as Linda. Neither woman was armed. If Cassie was going to take her down, she would have to use her hand-to-hand combat training and pray she remembered enough to subdue a woman on a crazed adrenaline rush.

Though her heart pounded like a jackhammer in her chest, Cassie schooled her voice into a soft, soothing tone. "Linda, I didn't come in here to hurt you."

"The hell you didn't. You knocked me down." Her gaze shot to the handgun in the far corner.

"I only did that to take the gun away before you hurt yourself or someone else."

"It's my gun. You have no right to come into my house and take my gun away from me," she yelled. "If I want to fire my gun in my house, that's my business. If I want to shoot that stupid lying portrait, I will, and no one can stop me."

"What's wrong, Linda?" Cassie hoped that getting Linda to open up would help her calm down. "Why are you angry?"

She pointed to the portrait. "He did this to me. I wanted my baby. My Abigail. That's all. She was so small. So sweet and…too early." Tears welled in the woman's eyes. "He wasn't even here when she came. I had her alone. I couldn't call. The phone line was down, and he wasn't here!" Tears streamed down her cheeks.

"What happened to your Abigail?" Cassie asked softly.

"She came a month early. Lots of babies make it, even when they come early." Linda looked down at her hands. "I held her in my arms, praying for her to cry. She never did. I held her as she slept." Linda's arms rose as if she cradled that baby.

"Where was Frank?" Cassie asked softly.

Linda's head jerked up. "He was with her. She came to Eagle Rock because she was pregnant with his child." Her face contorted with rage. "He brought her into my house while I was holding my sweet baby Abigail. He sat me on that chair and told me to be quiet and let him think.

"Then his whore's water broke on my living room rug. He took her into my bed and delivered her brat. He came out with a screaming, crying, healthy baby girl, took my Abigail and put the whore's child in my arms." Linda looked at her hands again, tears falling. "He took my Abigail and buried her somewhere in the yard. I've spent the past twenty years searching for her and can't find her."

Cassie's heart ached for Linda. The woman had lost her child and hadn't been allowed the chance to grieve. "What happened to the baby's mother?"

Linda's eyes narrowed. "She came out of my bedroom demanding her baby. I didn't want it, but she didn't deserve her. Frank was *my* husband, and our baby was dead."

"What happened?" Cassie prompted.

"She killed her," a deep voice said from the entrance to the room.

Cassie spun to face Frank Matson.

He held a pistol in his hand, pointed at Linda. "She was still holding the baby when she charged into Beth. Beth fell and hit her head on the corner of the coffee table."

"She was fine," Linda said. "She got up. Frank made me give her the baby. She sat in the rocking chair and held her for the longest time like this was her home, and I was the intruder." Linda snorted. "Then she said she was tired and wanted to lie down. Frank took her into our room again and let her sleep in my bed."

"She didn't wake up," Frank concluded.

Cassie's stomach roiled. Frank and Linda had stood by and done nothing while Beth had died. "Why didn't you take her to the hospital?"

"I didn't know she'd die. I thought she was tired from just having given birth." He shook his head. "I didn't know."

Linda snorted. "Tell her the truth, Frank. You didn't want anyone to know about your whore or your bastard child. Especially my father. You were set to take over the business. If my father had known you'd screwed around while married to his little girl, he'd have killed you. He sure as hell wouldn't have given you the business. So, Frank hid his indiscretion."

"And saved you from going to jail for murder." Frank's lips pressed together. "And I'm still cleaning up your mess."

"But now, you're just as guilty." Linda's lip lifted in a sneer. "Earl knew you'd hung that drywall over the secret room. At the time, he didn't care because he didn't know what you'd hidden back there. When your whore was found, you had to kill Earl to keep him quiet."

"To keep you from going to jail," Frank insisted.

"And the avalanche?" Cassie wanted to know.

Frank frowned. "You were getting too close." His hand shifted, the gun now pointing at Cassie. "You and your boyfriend just had to go to Idaho Falls. I had to do something."

Cassie shook her head. "It's too late, Frank. Everyone knows now. You might as well put the gun down and turn yourself in."

Frank's face turned red. "No. This was not my fault. I didn't kill Beth." He jabbed the pistol toward Linda. "She killed her. I just cleaned up the mess. It was her." He jabbed the gun toward Linda again. This time, it went off.

Linda's eyes widened. She glanced down at her chest, where a perfect round hole marred the front of her white blouse. Blood seeped out, spreading across the white fabric.

Linda looked up. "You shot me." She dropped to her knees. "All I wanted was to find my baby." She fell to her side, staring at her husband, her eyes open and accusing.

Frank looked at his wife as if he couldn't quite understand what he'd done.

Cassie dove for the gun, trying to knock it from his grasp.

He held firm to the pistol and backhanded her with his other hand, his knuckles catching her across her cheek.

She staggered backward and fell over an ottoman, landing hard on her ass.

"Look what you made me do," he said. "Now, I have to clean up her mess again, and you with it."

# CHAPTER 14

DRAKE HAD MADE good time getting to the fishing hut, speeding all the way. He smiled, thinking about his first meeting with Cassie and how she'd let him off on a warning. This time, she'd give him a ticket if she was the one pulling him over.

Margaret was just coming out of the hut carrying a fishing pole and tackle box when Drake pulled up in front of the shack.

Her eyes widened, and she started to duck back into the shack.

Drake dropped out of the truck. "Margaret, it's me, Drake."

Her face cleared, and she smiled. "Damn it. You had me scared for a minute."

He hurried toward her. "I need to know two things."

The older woman smirked. "Nice to see you, too." She lifted her chin. "Shoot."

"Did Greenway have a construction job in Idaho Falls right before the addition at the lodge?"

Margaret's eyes narrowed. "Rings a bell." She touched a finger to her chin. "Yes. Mr. Greenway sent Frank to manage it. It was a test to see if he could handle a project all by himself."

"And the crew?"

"All from Idaho. Also, a test to see if he could handle staffing issues."

"Did any of the Idaho crew move to Eagle Rock after they completed the Idaho project?"

"No."

He'd known the answer before she'd said it. And he knew who'd fathered Beth's child.

Margaret's eyes rounded. "It was Frank, wasn't it?"

"That would be my guess." He pulled Margaret forward and kissed her forehead. "Thank you and your beautiful mind." Drake spun and ran toward the truck.

"Any time. And if you want to go fishing, you know where to find me," she called out.

"You're on!" he yelled back as he climbed into the truck.

He drove even faster back to town than he had heading out, coming to a skidding halt in front of the sheriff's office. Cassie's SUV wasn't there. The sheriff was just climbing out of his service vehicle when Drake rolled down his window. "Where's Cassie?"

The sheriff looked around as if surprised her vehicle wasn't there. "I don't know. She was here when I went out on a call."

"Our killer is Frank Matson. Where can I find his house?"

The sheriff gave him the address. "I'm coming with you."

"I'm not waiting." Drake shifted into reverse and roared out of the parking lot, headed north out of town. He prayed Cassie had gone home to her ranch, not out to Frank's place to question him about the Greenway employees who'd worked the Idaho project. If she had, she'd be walking into a whole lot of trouble. The man had killed Beth. Then he'd killed Earl to keep him quiet, and he'd already attempted to kill Cassie and him.

Drake pushed the accelerator all the way to the floorboard, pushing Hank's truck over one hundred miles per hour. He was going so fast, he could barely slow down enough to make the turn off the highway toward the stately house perched on top of the hill. He powered up the concrete driveway and skidded to a stop before he cleared the shadows of the trees. The house was further up the rise.

Drake's heart plunged to his knees.

Cassie's SUV was parked in front of the house,

along with a white truck with the Greenway Construction logo printed on the side panel.

Drake slammed his truck into park and jumped out. Swinging wide, he came up to the side of the house with the fewest windows and closest to Cassie's SUV.

A movement on the front porch caught Drake's attention.

Abby Matson was inching up to the door, carrying a garden hoe like a baseball bat.

"Don't do it, girl," Drake whispered. Before he could do anything, the girl entered the house, leaving the door open behind her.

Hopefully, her father wouldn't shoot her. She would provide the distraction Drake needed to get inside and assess the situation.

Bending low, Drake cut across the front of the house, careful to stay below the porch and out of sight of the windows. When he reached the stairs, he didn't wait, didn't hesitate. He took them two at a time, treading lightly to make as little noise as possible.

"Daddy!" Abby cried out. "What have you done?"

"Stay out of this, Abigail. This is between the deputy and me."

"No, Daddy," Abby said. "You can't hurt Cassie. She's the only friend I have."

"I can't let her go. She knows too much."

"That you killed my real mother? That you killed Mr. Hensley? Jesus, did you kill your own wife?"

"What do you care? She never loved you."

"Because she wasn't my mother. You made her pretend to be my mother. No wonder she hated me."

Drake eased up to the front door, wishing he had a gun. Thankfully, Abby hadn't closed the door.

Drake peered inside.

As he'd suspected, Frank held a gun pointed at Cassie. Abby stood too near to Drake for him to effectively launch an attack on Frank.

Drake willed Abby to move forward and take Frank's attention further into the room.

Just past Cassie, a woman lay on her side, blood seeping from a wound in her chest. It had to be Frank's wife.

The woman moaned and moved, attempting to crawl away.

"She's still alive!" Abby cried. "You can't let her die."

"Why not? She means nothing to you. I can barely tolerate her."

"Then why did you stay married to her all these years?"

Linda moaned again.

Abby dropped the hoe and ran to the woman on the ground. "You can't let her die. Daddy, please!"

Frank now had his back to Drake.

Drake bunched his muscles and launched himself

into the room, snatched up the hoe and swung it hard toward Frank's hand holding the gun.

The metal edge of the hoe caught Frank's hand and jerked it upward as a shot was fired.

Frank spun in a complete circle and came back around, the gun still in his hand and blood dripping from a gash on his forearm. "Bastard. I'm going to kill you and your girlfriend for meddling in something that was none of your business."

"No, Daddy," Abby said. "You're going to put down your gun and turn yourself in."

Frank glanced toward his daughter.

Abby held a gun in her hand, pointed at her father. "I've always loved you, but I can't let you hurt any more people."

"I did it all for you, baby," he said.

"No. Don't put that on me," she said. "You did it for yourself. I won't take responsibility for your lies and crimes. Now, put down your gun, or I'll be forced to shoot you. And you know I'm a good shot."

"I taught you how to shoot," he said.

"Yes, you did. But I won't kill to cover my lies. I'll kill to save the lives of innocents."

"Then I guess there's nothing left for me to do but this." He lowered the gun.

"Drop it to the ground, Frank," Drake said.

The man looked straight into Drake's eyes. Then he jerked his arm up.

Drake dove to the side and rolled to his feet in

time to watch Frank plant the pistol barrel against his chin and pull the trigger.

"No!" Abby tried to go to her father, but Cassie grabbed her by the shoulders and turned her away from the carnage.

Sheriff Barron burst through the front door, breathing hard. "Holy hell."

Drake took the gun from Abby's grasp and handed it to the sheriff. "It's over. Frank's dead, but you might need an ambulance for Mrs. Watson—if she's still alive."

Cassie bent to touch her fingers to the base of her throat. After a few moments, she shook her head.

Drake pulled Abby and Cassie into his arms. "I'm taking my family back to town. You can question us there."

"Go," Sheriff Barron said. "I'll handle this."

Drake led the two women out to Hank's truck.

"I should take my SUV back to town," Cassie said.

Drake shook his head. "I'll get some of the guys to come out and bring it back. You need to come with Abby and me."

Cassie took one look at Abby's pale face and nodded. "Absolutely."

Drake opened the back door of the pickup and helped Cassie up.

She slid across to the middle of the seat and buckled her seatbelt while Drake helped Abby climb into the truck.

Cassie secured the seatbelt over the girl's lap, and then wrapped her arms around her. "You're going to be all right."

Abby looked into Cassie's eyes. "I know. It's just a lot to absorb. I have no family. No one."

Cassie lifted Abby's chin, forcing her to look into her eyes. "Wrong. You have me, and you have Drake. We'll always be here for you. We're your family."

"That's right," Drake said. "We're family."

Abby nodded, tears welling in her eyes. "But I don't have a father and a mother."

Cassie smiled. "No, but we found your grandparents. They will be beside themselves that we found their granddaughter."

Abby's brow wrinkled. "I have grandparents?"

Cassie nodded. "Drake and I have met them. They live in Idaho, and they are the nicest people. Oh," Cassie fumbled in her pocket for her cell phone. "And I have a photograph of your real mother when she was pregnant with you. Would you like to see it?"

Tears flowed from Abby's eyes. "Yes!"

Cassie found the photo and turned the phone toward Abby.

Drake's eyes burned as tears filled Cassie's.

Abby took the cell phone from Cassie's hands. She stared for a long time at the happy woman in the photo. "I have her hair," Abby said, touching her own silky blond hair.

"And her blue eyes," Drake said. "And your grand-mother has the same blue eyes."

Abby crushed the phone to her chest and let the tears fall.

Drake's gaze met Cassie's.

"Let's go," she said softly.

He nodded, closed the back door and climbed into the driver's seat.

The drive back to town was a silent one with a few hiccups and sniffles.

Drake pulled into the sheriff's department parking lot and shifted into park. He turned in his seat. "Where should we go? We can't keep Abby here, and my room at the B&B is too small."

"Let's take her home to the ranch," Cassie said. "Richard would like the company, and it's about time he met you." Cassie smiled at Drake, making his heart beat faster.

"Are you sure?" Drake asked.

Cassie nodded. "As sure as you are."

"That's pretty darned sure." He grinned and drove out of the parking lot, heading for the Double D Ranch.

"I'd like to have a moment with your brother when we get there," Drake said.

Cassie laughed. "Go easy on him. He's trying hard to fill my father's shoes."

Drake loved the sound of her laughter and how

happy it made him feel, despite the fact two more lives had been lost.

Whatever happened, Drake wanted to be with this woman and make her as happy as she was making him.

# EPILOGUE

LATER THAT EVENING, Cassie carried a tray filled with watermelon slices out to the back porch where everyone had gathered at Hank and Sadie's ranch.

Abby sat on the porch steps with Richard, Cassie's brother, as he plucked a tune on the guitar their father used to play on cold winter nights. The song was slow and beautiful. Not sad but peaceful, fitting the beauty of the Montana sunset over the Crazy Mountains.

Drake took the heavy tray from Cassie and laid it on the table along with the other desserts. Then he slipped his arm around her and pulled her close.

"Your brother already likes me. That's a good sign, right?"

Cassie nodded. "He's somewhat of an introvert. If he likes you, you've made a good impression."

"Good." Drake's arms tightened around her. "I

want to be on his good side when I ask him for your hand."

Cassie shook her head. "You're not supposed to tell me that you're going to do that. Besides, it's too soon for that. We need to get to know each other better before we commit to a life together."

"I don't need a piece of paper to prove my commitment." He nuzzled the side of her neck. "I'm fully committed, and I'll spend the rest of my life proving it by my actions. If you want time to make sure I'm the right guy for you, I'll give you all the time you need. I'm not going away. You are stuck with me."

She turned in his arms. "Good. I like being stuck with you."

Hank came out on the porch and announced, "I have a surprise for Abby."

Cassie stiffened. "I hope we made the right choice and that she's ready for this."

Drake dropped a kiss onto her forehead. "She's a strong young woman. I think she can handle this. I think she needs this."

Hank stepped to the side of the doorway.

Amy and William Anderson stepped out of the house onto the porch, their gazes searching the faces of all the people gathered around.

Abby stood, her eyes wide. "Are you…"

"Your grandparents?" Amy said softly. She

nodded, tears welling in her eyes. "You look so much like Beth." She opened her arms wide.

Abby stepped into them. Amy and William hugged her close.

Applause sounded from the men and women gathered to celebrate the success of the Brotherhood Protectors and the special operations men who'd come to help restore the Lucky Lady Lodge.

Hank stepped over to where Drake stood with Cassie. "You do realize what you did to help find a killer and reunite a family is just the kind of thing we do with the Brotherhood Protectors."

Drake nodded. "I get it now. And when the work is done at the Lucky Lady Lodge, I'd like to come on board with your team."

"Make that two of us," Grimm said.

"I'm in," Murdock.

Utah raised a hand. "And me."

Hank turned to Judge.

Judge frowned. "Hell, if they're in, so am I."

Drake laughed and hugged Cassie close. "Moving to Montana has been the best decision of my life."

"You found me," she said.

"No, you found me."

She laughed. "Speeding into my life like you meant it."

Drake kissed the tip of her nose. "It's a good thing I don't let warnings scare me."

# SAVING KYLA

## BROTHERHOOD PROTECTORS
## YELLOWSTONE BOOK #1

*New York Times & USA Today*
Bestselling Author

**ELLE JAMES**

YELLOWSTONE
# SAVING KYLA
BROTHERHOOD PROTECTORS

*New York Times & USA Today* Bestselling Author
# ELLE JAMES

# CHAPTER 1

Kyla Russell was done with killing.

Especially when her target didn't deserve to die.

Camouflaged as an Afghan male in a long white thobe, the ankle-length white shirt Afghan men wore, she stood on a street in Kandahar, Afghanistan, a pistol with a silencer attached strapped to her thigh. Beneath the thobe, she wore dark jeans and a dark shirt for night movement.

She'd pulled her long, black hair up and wrapped it in a dark turban like the ones worn by men in the city. To complete her disguise, she'd applied a fake beard, bushy eyebrows and dark makeup to make her appear more masculine and able to walk freely around the city of over six hundred thousand people.

Kyla had spent the better part of the day before studying her target, both through the windows of his home and by tailing him as he'd left for work and returned. What about this man made him toxic? Why had her government deemed him dangerous to the world?

She made it a priority to research her assignments, to find out about the persons she was assigned to eliminate. Prior to accepting her current mission, she'd reviewed the dossier her handler had given her for Abdul Naser Ahmadi and had done her own background check on the man via her connections on the internet and the Dark Web.

The dossier had listed Ahmadi as an arms trafficker, supplying American weapons to the Taliban. Nothing in Kyla's own research indicated the same. In fact, Ahmadi was like a black hole of information. All she could find was that he lived with his wife in Kandahar and worked at a local university as a professor of language and literature.

Kyla had no qualms about ridding the world of pedophiles or people who tortured and killed others for their race or religious beliefs. She'd taken out cult leaders who'd planned terrorist activities in the United States and some who were killers in foreign countries.

Some of her targets had been dirty politicians, selling secrets to US enemies, placing her country's military in jeopardy. Those targets, she'd taken out with no problem and no regrets. The world was a better place without them.

Kyla took pride in never completing a mission

without first understanding the target and the necessity of taking him out.

Ahmadi was not raising any red flags. Still, she planned to observe the man for a couple of days in case she was wrong.

Standing on a street corner, her back to the wall of a building, she casually observed Ahmadi at a local tea shop where he sat with another man. Maybe this was the reason for the hit—this meeting with Ahmadi's guest.

Using her cell phone, Kyla snapped a picture of the man and sent it to her contact on the Dark Web, who had access to facial recognition software.

Within minutes she was surprised to receive a response.

Jalal Malik CIA.

Kyla frowned at the message. *CIA? What the hell?*

Kyla sent the picture of Malik and Ahmadi along with a message to an old friend she'd known from her days in the CIA. A man who had access to more than he should.

Jalal Malik CIA…Legit? Clean?

Her contact responded several minutes later:

Born in the US to first-generation Afghans who escaped Afghanistan and Taliban rule thirty years before and earned their US citizenship. Malik speaks fluent Pashto and joined the CIA to give back to the country that saved his parents. Now working to uncover a mole in the US government, who is feeding information and arms to the Taliban. Ahmadi is his trusted informant.

With Ahmadi in her sights, Kyla could have picked him off any time that day and disappeared. However, she couldn't pull the trigger, not when her gut told her something was off. Ahmadi wasn't dangerous to the US. In fact, his willingness to help the US find the traitor within made him an asset and put him in danger of Taliban retaliation. Why had he been targeted for extermination?

She'd followed him home to ask him that question. By the time he'd returned to his home, darkness had settled over Kandahar.

Kyla ducked into the shadows of the wall surrounding Ahmadi's home, where she stripped out of the white thobe and trousers and tucked them behind a stack of stones. Then she pulled herself up and over the wall, dropped down into Ahmadi's yard and watched for her chance to corner the target.

That chance presented itself within the hour.

Ahmadi's wife had gone to the bedroom. Ahmadi stepped out his back door onto the hardpacked dirt within the stone wall to smoke a cigarette.

Kyla slipped up behind him, clamped her hand over his mouth and pressed a pistol with the silencer attachment to his temple. She lowered her voice and spoke in Pashto, "Tell me why my government wants you dead."

He stood still, making no attempt to fight back. "Who is your government?"

She nudged his temple with the pistol. "The same government who sent your guest at tea."

He nodded and switched to English. "Perhaps we are getting too close to the truth," he said in a whisper.

Kyla released the man and stepped back, her weapon trained on Ahmadi's chest as he turned to face her, his hands raised.

"I am not your enemy," he said.

"Then why would my government send me to kill you?" she asked.

He shook his head. "For the same reason I had tea with another citizen of your country. One of your own is playing for the other side and has sent you to do his dirty work."

"What do you know that would make someone put a hit out on you?" she asked.

"If you will not kill me, I will tell you what I told my guest at tea." Ahmadi's eyes narrowed as he awaited her response.

Kyla lowered her weapon. She could still kill him if he made a move to hurt her.

Ahmadi drew in a deep breath and let it out slowly before speaking again. "I received the name of the man who has been coordinating shipments to the Taliban. He goes by...Abaddon."

"Abaddon?"

The man nodded. "The meaning of the name is destruction."

At that moment, Ahmadi's wife called out in Pashto, "Are you expecting a delivery? A van just arrived in front of our gate."

Ahmadi glanced toward the house.

A knot of foreboding formed in Kyla's gut. "Call your wife to you."

Ahmadi frowned. "Why?"

"Just do it. Now." Kyla turned and slipped between the wall and the house.

Behind her, Ahmadi called to his wife.

Through the windows, Kyla could see Ahmadi's wife moving toward the back of the house.

Kyla slowed at the front corner and peered through the wrought iron gate at a dark van parked on the street. A door opened, and a man dressed in dark clothes and a ski mask dropped down.

If the mask wasn't enough to make her blood run cold, the mini machine gun he carried did the trick.

Kyla's pulse slammed through her veins. She spun and raced to the back of the house, where Ahmadi and his wife stood together.

Kyla glanced at the wall she'd scaled easily. Ahmadi and his wife would not go over it as quickly, dressed as they were in long robes.

In Pashto, she said, "Over the wall. Hurry." She bent and cupped her hands.

Ahmadi urged his wife to go first.

She hung back.

"Go," Kyla urged. "Or we all die."

The woman stepped into Kyla's palms. With her husband pushing from behind, she landed on her stomach and swung her leg over the top of the stone wall. She dropped to the other side.

Kyla held her hands for Ahmadi.

"No, you go first," Ahmadi said.

"No time to argue," she remained bent over.

Ahmadi stepped into her hands.

Kyla straightened.

Ahmadi pulled himself up to the top of the wall and reached down to give her a hand up.

She shook her head. "Go!"

He slipped over the wall and dropped to the ground on the other side.

Doors slammed open inside the house as the man in the black ski mask worked his way through the rooms. It wouldn't take him long. The house wasn't that big.

Kyla got a short, running start, scaled the wall and slung her leg over.

As she slipped over the top, she glanced back. The man in the black ski mask had just reached the back door and flung it open. Before he could see her, she dropped to the other side.

Her turban caught on a crack in the wall. Unable to stop and free it, she let it go, the ponytail she'd wound around her head shaking loose. She didn't have time to retrieve her thobe. It didn't matter. Without the turban, the disguise was useless. All she could do was run. She raced after Ahmadi and his wife.

They ran for several city blocks. The couple wouldn't be able to keep up the pace for long.

Kyla glanced over her shoulder. The man in black rounded a corner and sprinted toward them.

"Turn left," Kyla yelled to the couple. They did, and Kyla followed. "Keep going and find a safe place to hide. I'll take care of him." She stopped running and waited for the assassin to catch up.

Ahmadi and his wife turned another corner, zigzagging through the streets.

Kyla waited, her gun poised and ready. When the man didn't burst around the corner as she expected, she eased her head around.

Several yards away, the man was climbing into the van's passenger side. Once he was in, the van leaped forward, headed for her corner.

Kyla aimed at the driver's windshield and fired.

Her bullet pierced the window.

The van swerved and then straightened, coming straight for her position on the corner.

She fired again.

This time the van swerved and slid sideways into a building.

The man in the ski mask jumped out of the

passenger side and, using the door for cover, aimed his rifle at Kyla.

Knowing her pistol didn't have the range or accuracy of the shooter's rifle, she backed away from the corner and ran. She had to get to a better position to defend herself or get the hell away.

She was halfway to the next corner when tires squealed behind her.

A glance over her shoulder confirmed…the van was back in action and barreling toward her.

In front of her, headlights flashed as a small sedan turned onto the street. A man leaned out of the passenger window with a rifle and fired at her.

*Fuck.*

The bullets hit the pavement beside her. Kyla turned right onto the street nearest her and ducked behind the first home she came to. She circled the house, leaping over piles of stones and brick, and hid in the shadows near the rear of the home as the sedan turned onto the street. The van was slowing as it approached the corner.

As the van turned, Kyla aimed at the front tire of the van and popped off a round. The tire blew and sent the van veering toward the front of the house behind which she hid and crashed into the front entrance.

Kyla didn't wait for the driver to recover. She backtracked and ran back in the direction from which she'd come, zigzagging between houses, hugging the shadows as she went. Several times, she was certain she glimpsed the sedan.

She hoped Ahmadi and his wife had made good their escape. After she'd split from them, she was certain the attackers had been after her. They had to know she wasn't Ahmadi. Her long ponytail would have given her away.

Making her way through the darkened streets, she pulled off the fake beard and eyebrows, wincing as the glue proved stubborn. She couldn't stay in Kandahar. Not dressed as she was. The Taliban patrolled the streets day and night, looking for people breaking the newly enforced laws. She would be arrested or beaten for her lack of appropriate attire.

Not knowing exactly who the attackers were, she couldn't afford to be caught. If they were members of the elite team of assassins she was a part of, they would know they were chasing her—and they were aiming for her, specifically.

As of that moment, she no longer worked for the US government. She was now a threat to the people who'd trained and recruited her. They'd be looking for her in Kandahar. She no longer had the support to get her out of the country. If she wanted out, she'd have to find her own way.

*Double fuck.*

Kyla made her way to the edge of the city, moving quickly. She had to get out before sunrise. She couldn't trust anyone. People wouldn't be willing to help her. Not a lone female without male protection. Especially dressed as a Westerner in pants, not wearing the mandated black abaya.

As she arrived on the edge of the city, she paused in the shadows of a fuel station.

A truck pulled up, loaded with bags of onions, oranges and various other produce. From the direction it had come, it was heading out of town for an early morning delivery.

Kyla waited for the driver to fill his tank and pay the attendant.

When he finally climbed back into the cab and started his engine, Kyla made her move.

The truck pulled out from beneath the light from a single bulb hanging over the pump and slowly picked up speed on the road heading west.

Kyla glanced left and then right.

The attendant had returned to the inside of the station. No other vehicles were in sight.

She took off, sprinting after the truck, grabbed the side rail and vaulted up into the back, landing on a stack of bagged oranges. Adjusting several heavy bags, she created a hole and fit herself into the middle, out of sight of other traffic that might pass them on the road. She settled back, praying when they stopped that she could find a way out of Afghanistan and back to the States.

Once there, she'd use her nefarious contacts in

the Dark Web and her former colleagues in the CIA to find out what the hell had just happened.

THE BUMPY ROAD and the sway of the old vehicle must have lulled her to sleep.

When the truck slowed and made a couple of sharp turns, Kyla's eyes blinked, and she stared up at the sun beating down on her and the buildings on either side of the truck as it maneuvered into a small village at the edge of the hills. She guessed it was making a delivery stop, which meant she needed to get out before the driver brought the truck to a complete stop.

Kyla pushed the bags of oranges out of the way and scooted toward the tailgate. As the truck turned another corner, she dropped out of the back and rolled in the dust into the shadows, coming to a stop when she bumped up against a pair of boots.

# ABOUT THE AUTHOR

ELLE JAMES also writing as MYLA JACKSON is a *New York Times* and *USA Today* Bestselling author of books including cowboys, intrigues and paranormal adventures that keep her readers on the edges of their seats. When she's not at her computer, she's traveling, snow skiing, boating, or riding her ATV, dreaming up new stories. Learn more about Elle James at www.ellejames.com

Website | Facebook | Twitter | GoodReads | Newsletter | BookBub | Amazon

Or visit her alter ego Myla Jackson at mylajackson.com
Website | Facebook | Twitter | Newsletter

*Follow Me!*
www.ellejames.com
ellejamesauthor@gmail.com

# ALSO BY ELLE JAMES

Shadow Assassin

## *Delta Force Strong*

Ivy's Delta (Delta Force 3 Crossover)

Breaking Silence (#1)

Breaking Rules (#2)

Breaking Away (#3)

Breaking Free (#4)

Breaking Hearts (#5)

Breaking Ties (#6)

Breaking Point (#7)

Breaking Dawn (#8)

Breaking Promises (#9)

## *Brotherhood Protectors Yellowstone*

Saving Kyla (#1)

Saving Chelsea (#2)

Saving Amanda (#3)

Saving Liliana (#4)

Saving Breely (#5)

Saving Savvie (#6)

Delta Force Rescue (#15)

Dog Days of Christmas (#16)

Montana Rescue (#17)

Montana Ranger Returns (#18)

Hot SEAL Salty Dog (SEALs in Paradise)

Hot SEAL,Hawaiian Nights (SEALs in Paradise)

Hot SEAL Bachelor Party (SEALs in Paradise)

Hot SEAL, Independence Day (SEALs in Paradise)

Brotherhood Protectors Vol 1

### *Iron Horse Legacy*

Soldier's Duty (#1)

Ranger's Baby (#2)

Marine's Promise (#3)

SEAL's Vow (#4)

Warrior's Resolve (#5)

Drake (#6)

Grimm (#7)

Murdock (#8)

Utah (#9)

Judge (#10)

### *The Outriders*

Homicide at Whiskey Gulch (#1)

Hideout at Whiskey Gulch (#2)

Something To Talk About (#2)

Who's Your Daddy (#3)

Love & War (#4)

### Billionaire Online Dating Service

The Billionaire Husband Test (#1)

The Billionaire Cinderella Test (#2)

The Billionaire Bride Test (#3)

The Billionaire Daddy Test (#4)

The Billionaire Matchmaker Test (#5)

The Billionaire Glitch Date (#6)

The Billionaire Perfect Date (#7) coming soon

The Billionaire Replacement Date (#8) coming soon

The Billionaire Wedding Date (#9) coming soon

### Ballistic Cowboy

Hot Combat (#1)

Hot Target (#2)

Hot Zone (#3)

Hot Velocity (#4)

### Cajun Magic Mystery Series

Voodoo on the Bayou (#1)

Voodoo for Two (#2)

Deja Voodoo (#3)

Cajun Magic Mysteries Books 1-3

*SEAL Of My Own*

Navy SEAL Survival

Navy SEAL Captive

Navy SEAL To Die For

Navy SEAL Six Pack

*Devil's Shroud Series*

Deadly Reckoning (#1)

Deadly Engagement (#2)

Deadly Liaisons (#3)

Deadly Allure (#4)

Deadly Obsession (#5)

Deadly Fall (#6)

*Covert Cowboys Inc Series*

Triggered (#1)

Taking Aim (#2)

Bodyguard Under Fire (#3)

Cowboy Resurrected (#4)

Navy SEAL Justice (#5)

Navy SEAL Newlywed (#6)

High Country Hideout (#7)

Clandestine Christmas (#8)

### Thunder Horse Series

Hostage to Thunder Horse (#1)

Thunder Horse Heritage (#2)

Thunder Horse Redemption (#3)

Christmas at Thunder Horse Ranch (#4)

### Demon Series

Hot Demon Nights (#1)

Demon's Embrace (#2)

Tempting the Demon (#3)

### Lords of the Underworld

Witch's Initiation (#1)

Witch's Seduction (#2)

The Witch's Desire (#3)

Possessing the Witch (#4)

### Stealth Operations Specialists (SOS)

Nick of Time

Alaskan Fantasy

### Boys Behaving Badly Anthologies

Rogues (#1)

Blue Collar (#2)

Pirates (#3)

Stranded (#4)

First Responder (#5)

Blown Away

Warrior's Conquest

Enslaved by the Viking Short Story

Conquests

Smokin' Hot Firemen

Protecting the Colton Bride

Protecting the Colton Bride & Colton's Cowboy Code

Heir to Murder

Secret Service Rescue

High Octane Heroes

Haunted

Engaged with the Boss

Cowboy Brigade

Time Raiders: The Whisper

Bundle of Trouble

Killer Body

Operation XOXO

An Unexpected Clue

Baby Bling

Under Suspicion, With Child

Texas-Size Secrets

Cowboy Sanctuary

Lakota Baby

Dakota Meltdown

Beneath the Texas Moon

Made in the USA
Monee, IL
01 July 2022

98951545R00144